The Queen of Closets

By Preston Brady III

© Preston Brady III 2024 All Rights Reserved

A BlueCollar Chaps Gay Novel

Jordan Sam is a New Orleans millionaire, a Washington lobbyist and CEO of the Jordan Sam Group, the biggest anti-gay lobby on the Hill. His brainchild *Stay In* is moving towards passage in Congress and if it becomes law it would punish people who are openly gay in public. Jordan, a feminine, single man in his Sixties, has a secret desire for straight tow truck drivers. He's also a dimensions queen. There's no such thing as too big for Jordan Sam. While he confronts and denies media accusations that he is Gay, he and his staff create a flurry of legislation for their corporate and nonprofit clients designed to roll back Gay rights to the pre-1960's. After he by chance meets tow truck driver Cooper McNally, he settles into his double life until something happens that turns both of his personas upside down. As he pushes on with one anti-gay bill after the other, his personal life collides with his professional one, leading him to make the biggest decision of his life.

Chapter One

If Jordan Sam could convert all the lifelong hours he spent longingly gazing at masculine men, wishing he could break through the self-inflicted barriers against progressing such a desire, those hours would calculate into well over a full year of unfilled pleasure. It had become almost impossible to change that now because as an esteemed Washington lobbyist for over two decades he had become a household name in many circles. Jordan Sam Group was now synonymous with the slogan he himself coined: *Stay In*. Some very influential companies and nonprofits were fed up with the so-called gay rights movement. It had gone too far. The queers weren't satisfied with just being accepted if they didn't advertise it - no, they wanted it pasted all over billboards across the country with monikers such as "We're Queer and We're Here," and "Queers Are Everywhere." They wanted to get married, adopt children, to flaunt their perversion everywhere, and it was people like Jordan Sam who were hired to make sure they didn't. It was an uphill battle, but someone had to do it - and the millions of dollars it raked in each year for Jordan Sam Group didn't hurt either.

Jordan fashioned himself into one of the leading advocates of anti-gay legislation in the country. Of course the chatter about Jordan himself continued to fill social media, how a man so girly acting could not be gay. One of the common explanations was that feminine straight men do exist, as do very rare sightings of the vaquita porpoise in the Gulf of California. Everyone had seen the man at the party who had a soft, sweet voice and crossed his legs sitting on the sofa and was campy and limp-wristed with the best of them. And then, in walks his wife and three children and the speculation ends like the snap of a twig. He couldn't be gay - he's married to a woman and a father of three kids. But one problem with Jordan is now in his late Sixties he had never even bothered with a cover. He remained single and celibate, unless one counts your right hand and a smut flick as sex. As long as he publicly denied being gay then he simply would not be gay. In the beginning, he dared not try the downlow approach, meeting in secret with other men, because the eyes of the media, the world, were upon him. It wasn't that he was being watched 24 hours a day, but he was in the limelight enough that he couldn't risk his secret being revealed - and in such a ghastly way.

But that day standing in line at the convenience store was a different sort of day. The strange things running through his mind that morning scared even himself. He woke up thinking he was in heat. His mind raced as his head still laid upon the pile of pillows in his million dollar bedroom. People can't get in heat, he thought. Men are not dogs - or are they? I feel such a strong desire to be with another man, to please him, it's almost uncontrollable. But I have had these thoughts before and they went away as quickly as they entered. Now, it is different. I feel like I am at a crossroads in my personal life, chained by my professional one. I'm sure I will shake this. I cannot risk following through on my desires. I am a well-respected lobbyist, a multi-millionaire transitioning into my golden years. Sure, I made sacrifices, but they were worth it - are worth it. Mother always said *care more about what others think of you, because what you think about yourself will never get you anywhere.*

And then Jordan had a rare epiphany, which was ironic because he loathed epiphanies and ethereal, visceral things. His roots were planted in a deep south what you see is what you get philosophy. You had ideas and they came from your gut where they always were, not some sudden ahh-ha moment that supposedly came your way as a magical gift. But this idea was different, and he admitted for the first time in his life it might qualify as one of those moments.

When he turned around and laid his baby blue eyes on the working-class man in line behind him, he almost couldn't turn back around. He had seen lots of good looking men in his long life, but this one took his breath away. Cooper McNally might be dumb and young, but he had been around long enough in his thirty years to know he was considered more than average handsome and as many a gal had told him, sexy. He was definitely sexy in his navy blue work pants held up with an extra-wide black leather belt and a large rectangle belt buckle with a deer engraved in it. His white t-shirt was smudged with motor oil and ground dirt because he had been laying under cars all day, hooking them to his wrecker for towing around town. At 6'4 with sandy brown hair and green eyes he commanded the attention of almost any room he entered. His sized 18 weathered and dirty steel-toed work boots made him look like some lumberjack giant who had somehow graced the presence of all the ordinary mortals around him. Jordan knew he was the tow driver because he could see his truck in the parking lot, the engine still running. Then came his epiphany, spurting out of his pretty mouth before he could stop it.

"Oh hey. You're the driver of that tow truck outside, right?" said Jordan.

"Yep," replied Cooper. "That's me. Why you ask?"

"Well, I am having a problem with my car," he lied. "I am not sure I should risk driving it home. Even though I only live about a mile from here I am afraid it might sputter again and stall on me. Do you think you could tow it home for me?"

Cooper smiled and chuckled. "Well, requests are supposed to be phoned into the office and they dispatch a truck. It could be me or even another driver -"

"-I'll pay you a hundred dollars," whispered Jordan.

Cooper thought about it. "So it's only about a mile from here?"

"Yes sir," replied Jordan.

"Well, I'm not supposed to but a hundred dollars cash could fit real nice in my wallet right now," said Cooper.

When they walked outside to Jordan's car, it occurred to Cooper that he had seen this man before.

"You look familiar," said Cooper. "But I can't place where I've - on the local news?. You some kind of politician, ain't you?"

"Shhhh," whispered Jordan, looking around the parking lot furtively. "I am a lobbyist. But please keep that between us. You promise?"

"I reckon," replied Cooper, scratching his balls. "I ain't no gossip or anything like that. To be honest I ain't even sure what a lobbyist is."

"We look after you voters on behalf of large companies and organizations. Thank you," sighed Jordan.

"You wanna start your car and let's give it a listen?" said Cooper.

"No, please just connect it or whatever you do and let's take it to my house," replied the lobbyist.

"You know, you could drive it and I will follow you. If it stops running and won't start then I could tow -"

"No, please just tow it," replied Jordan, knowing very well his car would make it home.

Jordan watched as Cooper got on his back and hooked his car to the wrecker chains and winch, his muscular legs spread apart, framing something so inviting and beautiful bulging in between. His pants were smudged there, indicating he either satisfied a regular itch, a habit, or maybe it was something else, a subconscious caressing of himself, hoping to fulfill a need a man such as him definitely had to have on a daily basis. Now Cooper activated the automatic winch which slowly pulled the car onto the platform of the truck.

"Get in," said Cooper, startling Jordan who forgot he would actually be riding shotgun in the tow truck and not in his car. He couldn't get the passenger door open so Cooper walked around and put his hand on the door handle but not before Jordan had completely moved his hand off. Cooper's hand was massive and calloused, tinged with the motor oil of a working man and even that slight, quick brush up against the driver's hand sent a thrill into the lobbyist. Cooper seemed to catch it and frowned, wondering if he was imagining it or what. Inside the cab of the wrecker Jordan breathed in the scent of motor grease and the heat permeating off Cooper. He watched as his large hands took control of the steering wheel, his muscular biceps undulating which each turn of the wheel. He saw a few beads of sweat roll down Cooper's long brown sideburn and suddenly wanted to touch them, to smell it, to taste the saltiness of this man. He now realized his thoughts, his real emotions had taken control of his being and he was a little frightened of where it might lead him in the next few minutes but then he found himself thinking, I don't care. It's time for me to do what mother would have so not wanted: to think of myself first, and others last. Cooper sensed he was being scoped by the passenger but he was used to being looked at - it came with being a tall, handsome hunk.

"Are you married?" blurted Jordan.

"Divorced," replied Cooper. "It was my fault," he added. "I cheated on her. I deserve what I got."

Then, without thinking, Jordan replied in such a way he could have been taken for a gushy cocktail waitress.

"Any woman who would let a man like you go, would have to be stupid."

Did I just say that, thought the lobbyist. Yes, I'm losing my mind.

Now Cooper knew for sure. His semi-famous passenger was a fruit and probably wanted to give him some head. Then it occurred to him he might want a famous dude to do that. It would be bragging rights down the road. Yeah, I got blown by famous political lobbyist Jordan Sam. Nope, I ain't lying. I even snuck a pic. Here, look.

"Why thank ya," replied Cooper, taking his right hand off the wheel and letting it rest between his legs. It was a gesture that did not escape Jordan's attention, and he allowed his eyes to bravely linger there for several seconds, imagining what must be concealed under those greasy work pants, not that he would be able to pay homage to all of that. He was an amateur, a novice wanting to play in the big league.

The GPS interrupted the moment.

"Turn right at 400 feet. Turn right. Your destination is on the left."

"Whoa," said Cooper, pulling into the long, circular driveway. "So this is how the other half lives."

The other half lived in a sprawling two story Greek Revival mansion adorned with a row of six Doric columns across a palatial upper and lower veranda.

"Is it just you who lives here?" ask Cooper.

"Just little ole lonesome me," said Jordan, realizing he just played the sympathy card.

"Dang," said the tow driver. "It looks like twenty people could live there and not even see one another all day. Let me pull your car off."

The driver went through a routine he performed all day long, and in a few minutes he was done. He stood there and waited for his hundred dollars but it seemed Jordan had forgotten, so he cleared his throat and shifted on his feet, looking at his watch - all signals to the lobbyist that he wanted to be paid. Finally, Jordan got it.

"Oh," he exclaimed, reaching for his wallet. "I'm sorry. How stupid of me."

Cooper took the five twenty bills and stuffed them in his front pocket. Then he let his hand linger across his zipper for a bit, looking at Jordan, wondering if he was going to make his move. Finally, after about twenty long seconds the lobbyist blurted, "What time do you get off work?"

Cooper looked at his watch. "I got two more hours on this shift. Why, what you got in mind?"

Jordan looked around the neighborhood as if being watched and almost whispered. "Can you stop by when you get off work? If by the off chance anyone sees you here in the driveway just tell them it's about towing my car to the shop. Can you do that?"

"Sure," replied Cooper. And then making sure there was no misunderstanding, he added, "And I'm just lettin you do that one thing, right?"

Jordan was so excited he could barely reply. So he wouldn't have to make any kind of play and risk rejection or worse. The driver already knew. How could he not? *Any woman who would let a man like you go, would have to be stupid.*

"Yes sir, just that one thing," replied Jordan. "I will see you in a few hours."

"It might be a bit longer if I need to go home, shower and change clothes -"

-"No," interrupted Jordan, perhaps a little too anxiously. "Just come straight here like you are now."

"You like that, huh?" smiled Cooper.

"Yeah," replied Jordan, shyly lowering his head.

He watched as the tow driver hopped back in his truck and drove the circle around and exited the driveway. I can't believe what I'm doing, he thought. I just invited a straight man to my house with promise of "just doing that one thing," and the fact of the matter is I am not really good at that one thing. And from the looks of him he's way more than just one thing - he's a bunch of them all strung together. I need a drink. Jordan fixed himself a scotch, a beverage he did not take to in the earlier years but quickly learned it was the drink of choice amongst politicians and other men in high positions. And God forbid you make the mistake he made the first time he was offered a drink after becoming part of the elite circle over twenty years ago, and say yes, *with a splash of coke*. The snickering still echoed in his mind from time to time. He even determined that it was also considered lightweight to drink scotch with soda so he started off with water and then after so much trial and error found out scotch neat was the most hetrosexual way to go: straight whiskey. No ice. No girly crap. Drink it like a man. Now he drank it like a true man because he poured almost a full glass and gulped almost all of it in two fell tips of the glass. Now he felt the warmth of the liquor as it slowly made its way down his lithe body. He looked in the mirror over the bar. Even at his age he still retained a youthful mien, his smooth pasty skin undamaged by sun, his blue eyes still holding that spark he had in his youth. He knew he looked feminine but there was not much he could do about it. He was so used to the homosexual allegations he could fend them off now like a cowboy roping a calf. No one had any proof because he didn't play. He didn't go to gay bars or restaurants, did not patronize any establishment that was crass enough to hang a rainbow flag on their stoop. In fact, he couldn't stand homosexuals who wore it on their sleeve, especially all the politicians who grandstanded their homosexuality. Oh whoopee, you're gay! Now what do you want us to do about it - give you a great big old phallic trophy? The more they screamed like little pansy babies for gay freedom, the more he worked on his lobbying strategies to curtail their antics. *If I can't be openly gay then why the hell should they be allowed to do so.* Keep your queer little asses in the closet with the rest of us - and oh, I know there are a lot of us who prefer to keep this affliction we have, to ourselves. You just make it harder for all of us with your constant barrage of we want this, we want that. The worst of it all was the getting married part. Imagine, two men walking down an aisle, being pronounced man and man and then kissing, exchanging rings, trying to emulate what hetrosexuals have. Jealous queers, thought Jordan, pouring another drink. I will need to have a really good buzz by the time the tow driver gets here. Maybe then I can get past my inexperience, my limitations of addressing something apparently so massive it can't be concealed by a mere pair of loose fitting work pants. He walked to a downstairs bathroom and splashed his face with water and combed his short, brown hair. He wouldn't be able to stay up all night because he had an early flight back to Washington. The House was in session, and one of his keystone campaigns would be on the floor for discussion. Now, feeling a little drunk he walked to the downstairs kitchen and opened the refrigerator. It was almost empty as he had not found time recently to restock it. But lying on the middle shelf all by its lonesome was a sealed package of inch thick pork link sausage, one continuous link of shrink-wrapped meat. Feeling mischievous, Jordan fumbled around in a utility room and found a tape measure. He poured himself another scotch and then with a pair of scissors cut the packaging and took out the link of sausage. It was obviously well over a foot long, so he took the tape measure and stretched it out to 12" and then with a knife cut the sausage at that point. He actually glanced around in his own kitchen, to make sure no one was looking and then he inserted the sausage in his wide open mouth. He slowly moved his head down on the sausage, inch by inch and then when he had the sausage just barely half way down his throat he gagged furiously and quickly pulled the sausage out and flung it across the kitchen. He couldn't believe it. He barely got six inches in his mouth - not even six really - *almost six*. Houston, we have a problem, he thought. That tow truck driver is going to laugh, pull my head off and get away from amateur hour as fast as he can. Maybe I can tell him ahead of time, I can half-way blow you. Will that work? *A half a blow job?*

Chapter Two

"Sure, I'll take a bourbon and coke if you don't mind," said Cooper McNally, settling into a $5,000 leather recliner in the library of lobbyist Jordan Sam. He couldn't help but notice the fireplace was almost as big as the garage door at his apartment complex, and an oil painting on a nearby wall sort of looked familiar, so he got up while Jordan was making the drinks, and looked at the name scribbled on the bottom right. The name Matisse did ring a bell and he bet the painting was worth hundreds of dollars. But he was just an ole country boy from deep, way deep in the south, and folks didn't bother themselves with a bunch of artsy stuff, unless it was the birdhouses Elmer made, or the purty quilts sewed by Molly Ann Tanner of state-wide fame. Naw, country boys focused on women and work, in that order because *if they didn't get no women there would be no work*. Cooper started work early, at ten years old helping slop pigs and ring chicken necks, squirt the milk out of bloated cow teats and pick green beans and squash before the morning sun turned into an inferno of fireball hell over the fields and valleys of this Cajun Louisiana. By the time he was 13 he was kissing farm girls and feeling up their freshly sprouted chest bumps, taking those daily activities to his bunk bed each night, rubbing one out, sometimes two, as he visualized the beauties he encountered that day. As he got older he graduated to car mechanics, taught the trade by proud redneck country men who bragged more about the cooch they got that night than the fact that the catalytic converter needed to be replaced. It took a couple of years for Cooper to realize most of the talk was just fish stories, bragging about what they wanted to happen, talk to make them seem more alpha than the other guy. He also soon found out that the other guys could brag all day long, but as luck would have it the good Lord had blessed him with something down below that was mighty impressive to a lot of girls. Or so it seemed, at first. One even told him one night, they gave you a double dose down there. Maybe a triple shot. Now lots of men, especially in the subtropical south, have big'uns. Cooper wasn't one to check out the competition in the high school locker room, so he didn't know how special he was.

"You mean a lot of other dudes ain't hanging like me,?" he asked one date at the drive-in movies one night after she felt him up and gasped.

"Cooper McNally!" she cried. "Have you got a measuring tape? This'un one for the record books I thank."

It just so happened he did have a measuring tape, one, ironically, he never even considered using on himself. He retrieved it from his tool box in the back of the truck and handed it to Darly Sue and then unzipped again.

As she tried to grab hold of him to measure it, it kept throbbing and wiggling.

"Make it stop for a minute Cooper McNally. I caint measure a wild snake."

Cooper knew if he tried to make it stop it might go soft on him and the measurement wouldn't be true. So he grabbed hold of his pecker and said, "Now, Darly Sue, now!"

And while time was precious she pulled out the tape and put it upside Cooper. It was only at the eight inch mark so she pulled out more tape. At ten inches the tape still left Cooper's man head unmeasured at the top. She sighed and extended the tape more. Finally she had it extended enough to get a true gauge of what he was sporting. She saw the number but it was still hard to fathom.

"Cooper McNally," she said with excitement yet pronounced apprehension in her voice. He looked down at the measuring tape as she spoke. Then, they blurted together: "14."

"I caint believe it," said Cooper.

"Me neither," replied Darly Sue, scared as a rat trapped by an alley cat. "Oh my God!" she hollered. "I forgot I'm supposed to babysit the neighbor kids tonight. Hurry, get me home," she said, thankful she was quick on her feet and came up with a way to get out of this date with a hillbilly whose daddy must have forgotten to press the stop button on his throbbing penis.

He would have thunk being that manly would swoosh in the babes, but as it turned out it did the exact opposite. In a small town word spread fast. Sure, some of the gals gave him a first date because they wanted to see it at least once, to see for themselves. But once they saw it they went running scared, petrified by an appendage they were certain would go way far below their sweet spot. Finally, at the age of 24 he met Claire Brimsley, a clerk at a local auto supply shop. She was a pleasantly plump transplant from Yankee country and she immediately took a liking to Cooper. At first he was a novelty. She was able to almost fully address his needs under the sheets and they meshed and got married on the courthouse steps a month later. But then one day Cooper had a few beers and succumbed to the charm of a bar waitress down at Flannigans, who tried her best to please him but fell way short of the mark and then suddenly she quit Flannigans and moved on to another gig. So did Claire after half the women folk in town rushed to be the first to tell her that her man was humping around on her.

Now a rich, influential man wanted to explore his vast man region, and Cooper thought what the hay, I heard they are better at it than most women. Something told him this lobbyist Jordan Sam knew what he was doing. You don't get to be rich by being a dummy. And he likes me in my sweaty work clothes, unlike all the women who made me shower and be all squeaky clean so they could sniff my perfumed underarms and smell the sandalwood scent of my extra-large hairy rocks.

Jordan pranced into his study with two drinks on a silver tray, as if somehow that would make them taste better. He almost could not contain his excitement. This was the stuff that dreams are made of, the pinnacle of a storied career and life most people could only dream of.

"Alexa, dim lights," he cooed. Cooper was impressed and wondered what else she could do. As the lights darkened in the classic study lined with floor to ceiling cherry bookcases and little what-nots of candelabra and Chinese figurines, Jordan readied for the pleasure he would give the wrecker driver, and the thrill it would give him to perform such a rare act. The dark cherry wood floor was adorned with a $97,000 Tibetan Trellis Oriental rug, a gift but not a gift wink wink, from a Chinese client seeking less stringent import regulations in the U.S. Now Jordan let his gaze direct to Cooper, who was sprawled out in the recliner, pretending to be almost asleep. He grabbed a throw pillow from the couch and placed it at the feet of the driver. He sensed it was, without the need for further discussion, time to begin the ceremony. The drinks had been a waste of time. He looked down at Cooper's work boots and wanted to take them off. He slowly untied the laces and then removed the first boot. The driver was wearing white bobby socks and they were a little stained from the interior lining and the sweat they had absorbed for the day. The lobbyist took in the manly scent and moved his face down to the sock. He pressed his smooth face against the large foot and breathed in Cooper's smell. He took off the other boot and did the same as Cooper lay there, peeking through his almost closed eyes, waiting, hoping the gay man could satisfy his need in a way he had never felt before. Jordan inched up between the man's spread legs and placed his fingers on his belt, fumbling to unbuckle it, nervous and yet excited - this was like opening a holiday gift except twenty times more exciting. He knew he would find a large one beneath the fabric, and had even guessed it would be at least nine, maybe ten inches in length and slender with a large mushroom crowning the prize. With the belt unleashed he unsnapped the work pants and slowly pulled down the gold zipper. The man was starting to rise some now and Cooper increased his pace so as to unbridle the tool before it got too big to do so. He gently pulled the work pants down from the waist and the tow driver cooperated by lifting up a little so they could slide down some. Cooper saw his checkered boxer shorts now and could wait no longer so lowered his head and kissed the fly area. Now the tool began to really rise up and Cooper stared in amazement as it kept doing so, a sleeping, lumbering giant being invited out of the cave. Suddenly he almost stopped. Something was odd. But he had to know, had to see for himself and there was no holding back, no possible delay as took hold of Cooper's boxer shorts and slowly slid them down. When the underwear band reached the crown of the tow driver, Cooper gasped. He pulled down further and as the man was fully released from the boxers the tool bounced out like a diver from a springboard. Jordan almost cried out as the tool slapped up against his face upon release, so hard he was sure there was a red streak on his cheek. He was momentarily stunned. And then he had the full picture of what was there: something so large he couldn't believe it. Cooper peeked at the man as he saw the challenge that stood proudly before him. Now he decided to talk because it was all on the table now, no sense in pretending to be asleep anymore. A man of few words he said to Jordan.

"14."

At first it didn't register with the lobbyist. Is that some kind of code word of which I am not familiar, he thought? Then the weight of the one word hit him. 14. As in 14 *inches*. Oh no. I can't even do 6. He looked up at the driver and cast the most pathetic, sympathy-seeking eyes he could muster.

"I'll do anything if you'll just let me start out slow. It may take awhile - weeks, maybe even months but I promise with all my heart I will eventually get there. Will you do that for me? Let me start slow and then with practice be able to please all of you?"

For some reason Cooper was impressed by what the lobbyist just said. Maybe it was the fact he didn't pretend he could do it and then disappoint by trying and then giving up, leaving him to have to hand finish on his own. Or maybe it was that unlike the women before him, he had an actual plan, a proposal that possibly could work. He was a believer in practice makes perfect and anyway, he didn't have any better options.

"Okay," he replied gruffly. "Your first practice session starts now. We'll go twenty minutes and then pick up again in a few days?"

"Yes sir," replied Jordan, who then began his first practice, and as expected, reached the 6 inch mark and had to stop. But right before the session was up Copper patted him on the head.

"Try one more time, get it just a little more. And then the most wonderful thing happened: Jordan reached the 7 mark, or somewhere close to that. He and the driver knew it was better than the first attempt and with that Cooper patted him on the face and said good guy. *You did good, real good, buddy.*

Chapter Three

The flight from New Orleans to Washington DC was business as usual. Jordan sat in first-class, in his usual 1-A seat and was waited on by Marcie, who had seen the lobbyist on this flight dozens of times. Life was good and he was super-excited to be testifying before Congress this afternoon. Several Congressmen had already privately expressed their support for Jordan's *Stay In* proposal. All that was left was to complete the fashioning of the actual legislation and then bring it before the House and hope it made it to the floor for a vote. He didn't have any doubt the bill would eventually slide onto the floor like a Bolshoi ballerina nailing a pleshette. Never in American history was there a better time to be an ultra-Conservative politician.

It seemed appropriate that he should say yes this time to the offer of a glass of champagne by the flight attendant. While it might seem a little early to celebrate, Jordan felt confident all would turn out as he expected. Also, he was celebrating something else: his coupling with straight tow driver Cooper

McNally. It was the type of joining he could only dream of for years - over 60 years to be more precise. He will fly back to New Orleans tomorrow morning and see Cooper for the second time - shoot for the 8 mark, and this relationship actually justified the legislation he was pushing for his clients. He took a big gulp of champagne and thought I am a role model for the very thing I am promoting. *Stay in*. Do it if you want but don't put yourself on a world stage and try to force everyone else to look at you with a standing ovation. And don't *out* people either. I might have come out in the past but the fact some of these radical activists accuse me of being gay and try to force me to take an ad out in the New York Times reading: I am gay, makes me want to climb even deeper into the cloister. That's why I have included recommendations for legislation punishing those who out famous people without their permission. A $50,000 fine and up to six months in jail does not sound unreasonable to me - nor to my clients. Some of them want even stiffer penalties. Those activists want a gay movement - well, I will show them one. Keep calling me queer. That's fine. This *not a queer*, ha ha, will make you pay for it. There is nothing and I repeat nothing like a private pansy scorned.

The list of Jordan Sam clients would shock a lot of openly gay people: household company names who put out thousands of everyday products that would be impossible to boycott unless you decided to go live on a desert island and survive on coconuts and whatever fish you could manage to stab with a bamboo stick. And another thing: a lot of them would be surprised if they knew the real reasons why these companies supported Stay In and similar legislation that was sweeping across nearly every state in the nation. They thought it was because these company leaders and their esteemed board of directors and shareholders had personal distaste for the so-called homosexual lifestyle - as if all homosexuals lived one singular lifestyle. No, it went much deeper than that. The detractors did not doubt that most homosexuals were smart - very smart, so smart they had already begun to infiltrate the upper levels of corporate and political America. The true fear was real: homosexuals in charge of the country. A queer president - maybe even a queer vice-president along with the queer leader of this great nation. Throw in a queer Speaker of the House and you've got a triple crown Fagmocracy. And then slowly, Congress is overtaken by openly gay senators and representatives. The next thing you know the United States of America is being run by a bunch of queers, because queers are very smart and they know how to excel, to make money as if it were growing on trees, to further their agenda which is to put themselves on totally equal footing with hetrosexuals. The evangelical religious card was just a ploy to hide the real fright. That's what the leaders fed down to the common folk: it's against God's word, so they twisted the scriptures as best they could and rode with that, with an impressive amount of success because in the world today no one knew what was real anymore. They found a party line, a platform and clung to that like a baby to a teat. Jordan Sam was a master of indoctrination, and was born with that queer radar spoon in his little mouth. He discovered at an early age he could convince people of almost anything - on the fly, no rehearsal required. Family and friends came to recognize he had a talent for dry humor. He could sling out jokes that seemed so real that people would recoil and cover their mouths. Then came the wait for it moment and all would laugh and knee slap because this Jordan boy was, as cartoonist Thomas A. Dorgan coined in the 1800's, the cat's meow.

Jordan Sam freshened up at the Georgetown condo he kept while in the District, and soon was taxied to the capitol's south wing where he met with the committee considering his clients' proposal. He tried to keep his remarks brief because he had learned in the past these American leaders are very,

very busy and every minute they are in office count like the lives of Mayflies whose entire life consist of 24 hours.

"Stay in because America's children do not need to see you out," said Jordan. "America has made great strides in extending rights to homosexuals over the past five decades. People get it: you exist. People understand it and see it as a private matter. American people have for centuries defined love as between a man and a woman. Adam and Eve. It's a story from the beginning of time. The American people would like for you to appreciate the space they have granted to you. Embrace it, for it did not come easy. But at the same time you should respect the sanctity of traditional marriage, and be content with the phenomenal gift of your own private relationships with little or no interference from society. Stay in please. Stay in or pay the legal price for not doing so. It's that simple. Thank you ladies and gentlemen for your time today. Please let me know if you have any questions."

A smattering of applause erupted from the small committee. One of the representatives spoke:

"No, Mr. Sam. I certainly do not have any questions." He looked around the table. "Do any of you gentlemen?" They shook their heads. "Mr. Sam, your proposal has legs - good, strong ones that need to walk on the main floor of this Congress. I believe I speak for everyone here today that it will be presented. We believe the chances of passage in the House are above average. It will face a little opposition in the Senate but with a new President on the horizon we also have the caveat of veto, if needed. Thank you again sir, to you and the giants you represent, for we could not do all this without you, without them."

Jordan Sam felt like a little kid who had just been told he was going to Disney World next week, all expenses paid and he could bring as many friends as he wanted. He was actually trembling with excitement as he rose from his condo in Washington the next morning, and prepared for his flight home. After a glass of in-flight champagne he texted Cooper McNally: "Tonight?"

In about ten minutes the reply came back: "All 14 will be there. 8:00?"

Jordan giggled and replied: "Yes sir." *Now I know how it feels to be a schoolgirl bonding with her very first beau.*

Now he leaned back in his chair and stared at his phone
screen. He liked calling his man yes sir. It showed a certain
deference and respect for him. It cushioned the obvious fact
that he, Jordan, had far more money than his man, but could
lower himself down off that pedestal and give his partner top
billing. But hold on there Betsy, he thought. He's not really
your man yet. You just met and he's been to your house one
time. Yet there was something romantic about calling him my
man. And the fact that he was straight and Jordan had reeled
him in against all odds, was another reason to feel giddy, on
top of the bubbly giddy he was feeling right now. Even though
it was the beginning of fall but still burning up in New
Orleans didn't stop Jordan from cashing in on one of his
fetishes: Long Johns - thermal underwear. He texted Cooper
and asked him to wear some and Cooper texted back: As hot
as it is? And Jordan texted back: It will make me do it better,
so the tow driver dug deep into his piles of clothes and found
a pair of Long Johns. I'm not wearing a thermal shirt, he will
just have to be happy with the bottoms. When he arrived at
the house that night he was in for a surprise when Jordan
opened the door. The lobbyist was wearing a black satin tunic
over a white silk t-shirt, and black hot pants showing his okay
for mid-Sixty long legs. He was already holding a tray with a
bourbon and coke for the tow driver and a Tom Collins for

himself. He smiled and waved Cooper in with his free hand.
The driver felt obligated to whistle, so he did, to show his
appreciation for the lobbyist dressing up for him. Then
Cooper decided he would play this second session a little
differently. Right there in the foyer he took the drink off the
tray and downed it in one big gulp. He took Jordan's drink off
the tray and ordered him "Drink it down, babe." For some
reason this thrilled Jordan and he did as he was told. Then
came the unexpected surprise. The tow driver put his strong
hands on Jordan's tiny shoulders and lowered him to the floor.
Oh my, thought Jordan. He wants me to do it right here. Then
it occurred to him he had never pleased a man who was
standing but he thought it was a very good idea and watched
as Cooper unbuckled and pulled down his work pants,
revealing the thick cotton of the cream colored long johns
bulging with the wrecker man. It was already growing as he
put his face up to the front and took in the scent and feel of
the fabric. Something about the long johns stimulated him,
inspired him to be determined to do much better than the first
time. Now he slid down the underwear and revealed the prize
he had thought about even as he was speaking in the halls of
Congress. When Cooper was fully revealed, Jordan began his
descent, using his long tongue up and down the tool before he
did. Then something happened. Something amazing. He went

down, easily making his given 6 inch mark and then further, to the previous accomplished 7 mark and then Cooper moaned because the lobbyist was moving past his previous record and was going down, down more and then it dawned on Jordan as he was already at what he guessed was the 9 inch mark: *I can do it much easier when he is standing up.* Somehow having his head and neck in a vertical position as opposed to bent down 90 degrees in the horizontal position, opened up his throat and allowed Cooper to virtually slide in without much effort. Cooper was getting more excited as he realized the lobbyist had stumbled across some sort of sexual utopia, a self-revelation that helped him find his sweet spot. The tow driver slightly bent his legs and then gently slid in to what they both knew was a stunning homerun: at least 10 inches. Jordan stopped at that point, so excited he almost forgot to breathe but he did, he took a long breath through his nose and just froze in position, allowing Cooper to enjoy the depth of this feeling for as long as possible. Then, as if it could not get any better Jordan made a swallowing motion with his throat, causing a muscle tightness around Cooper and eliciting a guttural moan from him and only encouraged Jordan to do it again. Finally, when he couldn't stay down that far any further the lobbyist slowly rose up from the instrument and when he was completely off, the tow driver's legs began to tremble and then an eruption the likes of which Jordan had never seen exploded upon the walls of the tiny alcove and showered down like drops of snow before they freeze into flakes.

"Ahhhhhh, umm ahh - agh ugh-ahhhhhhhhhhhhh!" hollered Cooper, his face contorted into a manly sexual array of muscles in intense pleasure. Now the wrecker man leaned against the wall, panting like a satiated pit bull. He looked down at Jordan who was still on the floor, and shook his head in admiration.

"I don't think it will be much longer before you get your trophy," he said hoarsely. "I'm startin to like you, babe."

Jordan looked up at him and batted his eyes. "Just wait until next time. I have another idea that will make it even better."

"Don't forget, this one was your boy's idea," chuckled Cooper.

Cooper patted him on the head and then let his fingers run through Jordan's hair. He's obedient and I like that, he thought. I'll bet it won't be long before he's got me moving

in. Maybe this is the *being kept* stage of my young life. *I hear
most men have one.*

Chapter Four

The Jordan Sam Group was on a lobbyist roll straight into
the Halls of Montezuma and further, with the five member
staff supporting their leader Jordan with proposal edits and the
stringent timelines dictated by federal government
regulations. On this cool, autumn New Orleans morning
Jordan was feeling in the best of spirits because the next card
he was about to play for one of his major clients, was pure
gold. *Removing the Grooming* was causing a phenomenal stir
in Congress and elsewhere as this new legislation presented
by Jordan's firm aimed to identify and stop gay groomers
from operating freely in America's schools. Since there was a
very fine line between some primary grooming techniques
used by homosexuals, and what could be considered ordinary,
non-evasive behavior, it was important for the team to fine
tune the proposal being submitted to the House committee.
Jordan's client, Straight Ed, a multi-billion dollar educational
conglomerate, insisted on precise definitions and some of
them walked that balance between ordinary behavior and
possible grooming. It was Straight Ed's overall position that
any mention of homosexuality in elementary and secondary

school teaching was not only not needed, but constituted a subversive currying favor of the children, a mental rub down that encouraged the children to entertain thoughts and even consideration of homosexuality. Straight Ed wanted any and all references to homosexuality purged from all school books and not mentioned at all in curriculum teaching. They wanted full control of all school librarians, and a list of all new books being considered for a space among the stacks of their sacred learning institutions.

"A teacher should not even use the word gay in the classroom," said one Straight Ed representative before a congressional committee.

"What about if the teacher is reciting from the William Wordswoth poem "I Wandered Lonely as a Cloud," asked a committee member, and then recited the entry:

The waves beside them danced; but they
Out-did the sparkling waves in glee:
A poet could not but be gay,
In such a jocund company

The Straight Ed representative thought for a moment and replied:

"The teacher should substitute the word gay with happy. The word gay has been hijacked by homosexuals and therefore has no further usefulness in poetry and literature. All books must be vetted before being allowed in any school in America. *If God created these infiltrators of our great democracy then shame on you God! I guess even God can make a mistake!"*

Unfortunately, the Straight Ed representative was unable to continue his speech. The applause in the chambers drowned him out.

The next day Jordan was back to the District grind. It was a mostly successful day, with some admirable progress for the Stay In bill.

That evening a nice crowd gathered at Filibuster's, a posh bar near the capitol where it was always happy hour for members of congress and their guests, and where a house rep with a male companion bumped into Jordan and greeted him.

"Your firm is fabulous, just the cream on a Boston cream pie," he said, a drink in his right hand and the wrist of his left hand so limp it almost seemed it was double jointed.

"Why thank you," replied Jordan, scanning his masculine companion who was wearing Carhartt pants and a Polo shirt.

"Oh, silly me," continued the representative. "Jordan, this is *Rod*ney. He's my security detail."

"Really?" replied Jordan.

The representative winked. "See, we can *stay in* and still be social."

"How clever," said Jordan, thinking *he knows*. "I'm glad we ran into each other. Nice meeting you Rodney. You two have fun. Take care."

Later that evening Jordan revisited the brief meeting in the bar. That representative had proved you really can have your cake and eat it. *Security detail*. He absolutely loved that. Then, the thought of perhaps one day actually bringing Cooper out with him sometimes, grew legs. I mean if it gets that far. I mean if I get that far. I still have several inches to go.

The next morning Jordan was back in the Crescent City, hardly able to stop thinking about Cooper. He really needed him to come over that night. But Cooper decided it was time to play a hard to get card, to make his babe sweat a little. It turns out cunning gay men don't sweat. Jordan called him.

"8:00 sir? Remember I have a new technique up my sleeve. You will love it," said Jordan.

"Awe," replied Cooper. "You not going to believe what happened this morning. I mean you won't believe it."

""What?" replied Jordan. "What won't I believe?"

"I towed this broad. She's from Florida. Anyway, she was pretty freaky if you know what I mean. She didn't hold back and next thing I know I told her how I got head standing up and she said that's so cool because that's something they teach in the sex education class she is taking. So I kinda laugh politely and say something like yeah but do they teach you how to wolf 14 and she didn't miss a beat and said yeah she already passed that test."

"Huh?" replied Jordan.

"Yeah," said Cooper. "Then I grabbed myself down there and was just joking when I said *14 calling for proof* and guess what she said?"

"What?" said Jordan, on the edge of his seat.

"She said ' this proof is in the pudding gal wants you in her kitchen tonight. In her opening act she makes a baseball bat disappear'."

And then there was no reply from Jordan so after a long thirty seconds Cooper continued.

"Jordan? You there?"

"I-I feel…like I might faint…oh, my head feels so light…hello? Hell-oooo?" whispered Jordan.

And then the line went dead. Jordan tossed his phone onto the sofa, popped up from his seat and pranced over to the bar and poured a neat scotch, a reward for the outstanding performance he just gave. If that straight hillbilly thinks I'm going to fall for the "this woman wants me so bad" routine, then he don't know Jordan Sam. The phone rang again but Jordan didn't even look at it. He knew who was calling. But after it kept ringing every few minutes and he was feeling the warm effects of the scotch, he answered, sounding sleepy.

"Hello?"

"Hey, did I wake you?" replied Cooper. "Sorry, I was calling - something happened -"

"Yeah, I dozed off," lied Jordan. "And I had a strange dream. You were in it and you had met some woman and she had a measuring tape and baseball bat in her hand and - and a Birthday cake and - and - I don't know. It was really more of a nightmare…"

"Yeah, that sounds like a bad dream," replied Cooper. "Are you want'in me to drop by tonight?"

"Is the Pope Catholic?" replied Jordan.

"I reckon,"said Cooper.

"Well, he is," giggled Jordan. "Yeah, same time. I got a new technique to try on you. I think it's going to drive you wilder than you already are. Take a shower but put back on your dirty tow truck clothes."

"Huh?" said Cooper.

"Don't huh me mister. You know what I like," said Jordan.

"Yep," replied Cooper. "You like your man in his hot and sweaty working situation."

"One day Imma gonna walk up on you standing by your truck in the woods somewhere and accidentally drop my phone right in front of you," said Jordan.

"Be careful," replied Cooper. "There might be a big snake nearby, one of those kinds that strike your throat real quick."

"You are more clever than I even thought," cooed Jordan.

Yep, thought Cooper. And I also snore real loud but you don't need to know that until after I move in.

Since he had some time to kill, Jordan went into his home office and worked on parts of the new legislation several of his clients were proposing. There was considerable agreement from the more conservative members of the companies and nonprofits that there should be laws requiring all Americans, from birth and moving eternally forward to abide by their birth sex. The clients wanted the bill to have specific passages that prevented circumventing the law, such as what Jordan's firm decided to call *Birth24*. Birth24 stated:

All citizens at all times, regardless of age, race, creed, or color shall present in public their true native birth sex. Any deviation from this can be punishable by law, resulting in on the first offense up to six months in prison or a juvenile facility in the case of minors. Additional offenses can result in up to three years in prison or similar facility. This law applies even in the case of costumes for entertainment purposes, unless such display is performed in a registered and recognized theater and said characters were previously written into a script prior to this law. Such exemptions must occur on a stage as defined by the Theater Association of the Americas.

God, I'm good, thought Jordan as he was editing the passage. I wrote this - *me.* To my detractors - this is why I am a multi-millionaire. I have talent and I have vision. Just because my vision does not congeal with your gay transgender billboard mentality does not lessen my genius. There, I said it: genius. I'm not embarrassed to recognize my gift. People are like flocks of birds and flocks have leaders and leaders tell people how to behave, how to live. Those people who fall out of the flock will be punished. To all those people who think they have some special freedom when they are born and that they can just live their lives however they want, well, Jordan Sam et al are here to tell you that you are dreadfully mistaken. Fall in line - that's what you will do: *Keep in step, toe the mark, Come to heel, Follow norms, Fold up, Throw in the sponge, Knuckle under, wave the white flag, be submissive.* And speaking of be submissive, I'd better tidy up and get ready for Cooper coming over tonight.

Before he drove to Jordan's tonight Cooper McNally had a good idea. He showered and put on his dirty work clothes.

Then he slid under his tow truck and fiddled with the screw on the oil pan and let some oil spill onto him. Then he got up, wiped his right hand across his shirt and then grabbed his nether region and rubbed. There, he thought. That should make him wag his tail.

When he walked through the front door Jordan noticed right away and raised his eyebrows in appreciation. "You need to be on a bus stop billboard so women can go crazy over you."

"What about the men?" replied Cooper.

"As long as they do it in private and don't publicly gush all over your poster, I'm good," replied the lobbyist. "Come into the study and plop back in your chair," he continued.

"Oh, it's my chair now, huh?" chuckled the tow driver.

"Yes sir, it's yours," agreed Jordan. "Now, let me make you a drink and me, I'm having a cup of hot tea."

"Hot tea?" laughed Cooper. "Will it be spiked?"

"Nope," said Jordan. "You will see why in a minute."

After Jordan handed Cooper his bourbon and coke, he grabbed a throw pillow from the sofa and put it in front of the recliner. Then he took a big drink of hot tea but didn't swallow it.

"Hmm," said Cooper, guzzling his drink. "You gonna swallow that?"

Jordan swallowed the tea and before taking another drink replied, "That's what he said."

With hot tea still in his mouth the lobbyist began unzipping Cooper, not even bothering with his belt. Now he fumbled to get the tow driver loose from the confines of his work pants, taking note of the abundant motor oil streaks all along the zipper area. Cooper's snake started warming to the attention and once it was freed through his boxer short's fly it continued to a full salute to him who was paying homage. Then, Jordan swallowed the hot tea that had been in his mouth for almost a full minute, and with his free hand took one more big gulp, swishing it around in his mouth as Cooper watched and wondered what was next. Soon he found out. With his mouth almost hot from the tea routine he went down on the wrecker driver. The minute his mouth had him Cooper moaned because now he got it: his tool felt so warm in the lobbyist's mouth, and now he was showing his experience from the previous sessions and already at the 10 inch mark. He knew he would have to stand to allow Jordan to maybe get some of the rest so he put his hands on Jordan's head.

"Stay with it," he said. "I'm standing up."

The driver slowly stood, keeping his hands on Jordan's head so he wouldn't come off of it. The heat of his mouth was driving him wild and now standing he gently, slowly guided the lobbyist further in. At first there was a little cry from Jordan but then he exercised mind over matter and kept descending. Suddenly he bobbed down the rest of the way, only for a few seconds and then came back up to the 12 inch mark.

"Ahhhhh," you did it," moaned Cooper. "I'm proud of you. Here we go…"

The lobbyist came up and readied for what he already knew would be a 4th of July display of cream-tinted technicolor, and he was right. Cooper went flying across the room, landing on the coffee table which was a good four feet away. Now he used his hand to help guide his bottlerocket, sending sparks up and then down onto them, Jordan, his mouth wide open in awe and raw excitement. A hallmark had been reached. Cooper patted him on the head.

"You did it, buddy. You damn did it. The first," said Cooper, looking down on the gloating lobbyist. Then Jordan stood up and pranced towards the study door.

"Follow me, mister. I want to show you your room."

Chapter Five

A few months after Cooper McNally moved in with Jordan, the lobbyist was already calling him Coop and giving him back rubs and massaging his giant feet, sometimes kissing them to show the depths of his affection. One night he even sucked one of his big toes, but after a small piece of toe jam dropped into his mouth he stayed away from that pleasure. Not long after he was settled in Jordan told him "Give your notice at the towing company. You can be my private mechanic.."

"Sure thing," grinned Coop, but your car never has any problems so…"

"Sooo, it will have to from time to time because you ain't moving in here and turning into a pansy white-collar guy. I want you to stay working-class, and you know I love you in your greasy blues."

"Yeah, you sure do," agreed Coop. "Hey, I was in our workout room earlier this morning. You wanna sniff under my arms?"

"You think of everything," replied Jordan, lifting Coop's t-shirt and burying his face into his hairy, sweaty armpits.

"I probably shouldn't brag on this," said Coop, watching Jordan, "but my birthday is on January 1st. I turn the big three O next week."

Jordan bolted up from under his arm. "What a way to start a New Year," he said. "I will just have to think of something to get you…"

It was then Cooper decided it was a good time to move their relationship up a notch. He pulled Jordan onto him as he sat in his recliner. The lobbyist feigned protesting but in his mind he was thinking oh my, *this is how straight people do it at home*. Then Cooper took his strong, calloused hands and pulled Jordan's face to his. Now they were face-to-face and Jordan couldn't believe it. Is he going to? Is he? I can't believe it. And then he did. Coop pulled Jordan closer and gently kissed him on the lips. It wasn't a long kiss and there was no tongue involved but it was a kiss from his man and Jordan was screaming to himself inside, *I'll take it, by damn I will take it!*

That wasn't so bad, thought Cooper. A pair of lips is a pair of lips. I closed my eyes and it could have been Taylor Swift or Beyonce. Now Jordan hopped up and it was easy to see he was in a very good mood.

"Imma run real quick and go get us some beignets and chicory coffee," announced Cooper. "I'll take my old pick-up truck," he added.

Are you sure?" said Jordan? You can drive the Jaguar."

"Naw, I need to drive my truck once in a while, keep it running," he said.

But in a few minutes he came back inside and found the keys to the Jaguar. "Dang, he said. "It wouldn't crank. I'm thinking it's got a transmission problem."

And my Birthday is next week and if you need any ideas about what to get me, well now you know, thought Coop.

Suddenly, Jordan spun around from dusting a bookshelf and made an announcement.

"Now that you won't be towing cars anymore I've got a new job for you!"

"Yeah? What's that?" said Coop.

"Security Detail," replied the lobbyist. "You will be my private security detail. And your first assignment will be on your Birthday slash New Years Eve. We're going to the American World Family bash at the new Le Arrondissement Hotel on Canal Street."

"Cool," replied Coop. "Are those the people you work for?"

"Yep," said the lobbyist. "Almost all the people my firm lobbies for will be there. But you are my security detail. *Just* my security detail, if you know what I mean."

"Sure thing," said Coop. "Who am I protecting you from?"

"That's easy,"snickered Jordan. "All the screaming fairies and their ilk. Your job is to help push them back into their little lavender and rainbow colored closets and keep them away - far away - from moi."

"What's a moi?" said Coop, puzzled.

"Dang you Coop. I'm going to have to fly you to Paris one day when Congress is in recess. Moi - me, baby. Me."

Normally Congress would still be in recess until after the New Year, but several of the more conservative committees were still having limited meetings because as one of them put it, the future of the American Family is at stake. We can take no holiday from saving it from destruction. And, he added, the Jordan Sam Group is doing a stellar job with the lobbying efforts they have presented on behalf of American businesses and organizations. They scheduled a Zoom meeting with Jordan and he took the call in his home office.

"Gentlemen, I think you will be pleased to hear of a new project developed by my firm. It addresses the rights of family owned restaurants across our great nation. These hard-working folks have for years expressed their frustration at having to cater to openly, blatant homosexuals who enter their establishments in extreme behaviors of man on man or woman on women public affection. These people do things such as enter establishments holding hands, kissing as little children watch from their tables. Then as they dine they perform such actions such as kissing each other across the table, staring at each other, holding hands, displaying a public affection that frankly has caused undue distress upon the children of America. The legislation I present to you in this regard is called *Stand Your Table*. Stand your table will allow restaurant owners to legally refuse service to openly homosexuals, and to display discreet signage that will provide fair warning to such couples that overt behavior legally does not have to be tolerated and the owners or their staff can require such a couple to leave the premises should it become necessary. Gentlemen, you will see the final form of this proposal post haste following the holidays."

A murmur of approval flashed across the Zoom screen and Jordan smiled.

"Jordan Sam," said one of the committee members. "I frankly do not know what American families would do without your firm being in existence. It's like the good Lord looked down on our great nation, scratched his head and said 'there's something missing, something…yes, a company that can help promote my work, help my flock. I hereby christen Jordan Sam to be that person. Amen'.'"

Now the Hollywood Squares Zoom screen erupted in good natured chuckles and a few clapping hands. Jordan felt a surge of pride rise up his spine and when it reached his old but still pretty face it flushed a rosé tone that caused his baby blue eyes to sparkle. He never felt so needed, so pure.

"Why thank you for such a compliment sir. I am here to tell you my company is only getting started - just getting this thing going. Stay tuned for better things to come. There is nothing I am more proud of than protecting the American family."

And being the first person to take all 14 of Coop McNally.

The next day Jordan was still riding high off the praise he had received from the committee and was in a big shopping mood so he drove to a truck dealership to buy his man a brand new Jeep Gladiator High Altitude and pay cash, which thrilled the salesman but attracted a walkover by the general manager who suggested he finance through their dealership. It appeared the manager wasn't going to allow the cash sale so Jordan smiled and looked him straight in the eyes.

"Have you ever heard of Stay In - the congressional bill being reviewed by Congress right now? It's been all over the news so you couldn't miss it. Well, that's me. *I wrote that.* I can see from the ring on your finger that you are married, and a man like you probably has a house full of kids. I'm the guy saving your kids from flagrant homosexuals. I suggest you write up the bill of sale so I can get back to saving your babies."

The manager smiled and looked Jordan up and down as if he were bruised fruit on sale in the produce section.

"Yes, you are correct - I am married," he said. "Married to my husband of 5 years. And yes, you are also right: we have a kid. Tony. We adopted him last year, although we started the process over 3 years ago. Thanks to closet queens like you we had to jump through 20 hoops of fire and chop off one of our arms to get through the process. Now, please listen carefully because I'm only going to say it once. You can take your $55,000 of tainted cash and priss it right off this showroom floor, and as my mama used to say, don't let the door hit you in the ass on the way out. Shoo."

Jordan looked at the man with the most evil face he could muster, but turned around and walked out the door. He couldn't afford a scene. He was in shock at the audacity of that man. Mental note to self, he thought. Create a bill that prohibits openly gay people from working at car dealerships. At the next dealership he was able to seal the deal and requested for the Jeep to be delivered to his home on New Year's Eve. Cooper was going to be so ecstatic. I didn't spare any expense for him. If he stays around long enough, and kisses me one more time I swear I will hold on to that man for the rest of my life. How many guys like me have a man with 14? Almost zero because I looked it up and less than 0.5% of the men in the entire world have 14. *That's hardly any men.* Almost zero. But my man does. My man is 14 long and he's handsome and straight and everything I've wanted in a partner.

A few days later while they were sipping cocktails and getting dressed for the big gala at Le Arrondissement Hotel,

Jordan received a text that the Jeep with the driver was in the driveway.

"Come Cooper, follow me. Your birthday present is outside."

"Huh?" replied Cooper. What, did you buy me a riding lawnmower? So that's why you got me here, to be your lawn boy."

"You'll see," fluttered the lobbyist, dressed in a cream tuxedo with sepia colored bowtie. Cooper was just in his tux pants and shirtless. "Do I need to get dressed?"

"No mister, come, follow mother."

When they got outside Cooper's mouth dropped as he saw the shiny new silver Jeep. A man was standing next to it holding the keys and paperwork.

"That's for me? Wow!" hollered Cooper, and not even thinking or caring ran up to Jordan and picked him up off his feet and twirled him a full rotation before dropping him and planting a big kiss on his lips.

"Cooper, is that you?" said the young man standing with the Jeep.

Cooper froze. Jordan froze. They looked at this man who just addressed Cooper by his name. Cooper moved in closer. Then he saw it. What's his name? Wiley, yep Wiley - the gay dude who worked for the tow company as a dispatcher about two years ago. Now Wiley approached him and hugged Cooper.

"Man, I didn't know I mean I had no idea - zero. How cool is this?" said Wiley.

Cooper looked at Jordan and Jordan was biting his nails.

"Well bro, it's not exactly what it looks like I mean-" started Cooper.

-"I know what I just saw," laughed Wiley. "Hey man, it's cool. I ain't telling nobody. I can see a guy like you wanting to keep it on the downlow and all."

Jordan stepped up and took control of the situation. When he started speaking Cooper frowned. He had never heard that voice come out of Jordan.

"Now look here buddy," he addressed Wiley. "It don't bother me that Coop is the way he is and apparently has some kind of crush on me," he said hoarsely, trying to sound like a masculine straight man.

"My wife and I are allowing him to stay here until he gets back on his feet. We are not prejudiced but we suggest you respect Cooper's privacy and not tell what you saw tonight to anyone - right Cooper?"

Cooper looked at Jordan so confused he almost couldn't reply. And then he looked at the $55,000 Jeep and thought hey, I will go along with almost anything at this point.

"Yes sir, Mr. Sam," said Cooper. "I'm sorry I threw myself on you. You've asked me not to do that before. I promise it won't happen again."

"Very well, Cooper. Now, sir, please give me the keys and paperwork and it looks like your ride is just pulling up," said Jordan.

"Yes sir," said Wiley - please sign here, and here, and one more place -here. And oh, sorry Cooper. No, I won't say anything man."

And then Wiley got in the car with the other driver from the dealership and started giggling. "Man, you won't believe who just picked up another man in that driveway and twirled him around like they were on the deck of Love Boat - and then kissed him."

"Who?" said the driver.

"Cooper McNally," said Wiley.

"The Cooper from the towing company where you worked and who used to pull cars for the dealership? That dude? You gotta be wrong. He's the straightest most redneck Skoal chewing country hick I ever seen in my life."

Wiley laughed and slapped his knee. "Ain't it funny how straight can bend a little bit when the words sugar daddy comes into the picture?"

"Dang," said the driver. "I wished I had a sugar daddy. My rent is due tomorrow and I might have to let that old dude blow me again just to get a little help."

"The one that bites?' laughed Wiley.

"I've still got battle scars to prove it."

Looking like an elegant gay couple but not thinking so themselves, Jordan, with Cooper behind the wheel pulled the new Jeep into the valet park of the Le Arrondissement Hotel. Jordan had coached Cooper on the way.

"Don't stand next to me - stand off to the side of me. Not directly behind me - to the side. You are protecting me, scoping for possible aggressors," he instructed. "Always have your arms down the front of your body, folded, and your eyes gently scanning the room. Don't put your hands in your pockets, unless you have to briefly scratch your balls. You can't scratch them publicly here - it would cause a minor scandal. Here, I got you an earpiece. Don't worry, it's not connected to anything. It's for show. It gives the appearance you are listening to a network or dispatch team, ready to receive information regarding any suspicious people in the building. I won't be introducing you to anyone except for the few bold, extremely noisy ones who won't be able to enjoy the party unless they get their fix of gossip. At that point I will nod in your direction and just say 'This is Cooper. He is my security detail.' That is not a cue for you to bounce over and join in on the conversation. You are low-key, background fuzz - oh, I just made a double entendre. Well, sir, any questions?"

"Sounds like a lot of fun,"replied Cooper wryly. "Happy birthday to me, huh? So basically, stand there and don't have any fun, just pretend to be your bodyguard."

"Mister!" cried the lobbyist. "At least you get to go."

"It was definitely at the top of my bucket list," replied Cooper. "Attend a big party where everyone is munching on snow crabs, drinking champagne and losing themselves in animated and witty conversation, and just stand there and watch it all."

"You can sneak a few o'dourves," replied Jordan. "I've seen G-men do it in the movies."

"Gee, thanks,"said Cooper as they arrived and relinquished the Jeep to a valet.

The minute they entered the grand lobby of the French-styled hotel, other guests began flitting around Jordan like hummingbirds on a feeder.

"Darling," said one man to his wife,"this is the man I have been telling you about - Jordan Sam. He is going to make America straight again."

"My immense pleasure," said his wife, extending a hand for Jordon to kiss. "Mind you, we're not anti-homosexual," she said. "We just think there is a time and place for that sort of thing. *Those people* deserve some freedoms. Why I was telling Charlie wouldn't it be great if they could *all* go back to San Francisco and just let that be their place."

"That is a marvelous idea," replied Jordan, immediately regretting the use of the adjective because he realized it sounded so gay. "That is definitely something my company could research for feasibility. If we had them all in one place, then it's like they are happy and we are happy. We don't have to, um, bump into one another," he laughed.

"Charlie, I love this guy," she replied, taking a sip of champagne.

And so it went for the next half an hour, seeming to Jordan almost as if this party was in his very own honor. It confirmed his belief that the people who work behind the scenes of national legislation do get noticed, and are recognized. The fact they are not plastered all over the news every day did not take away from the fact that without lobbyists there would be no solid legislation to protect America. Everything was moving along as smooth as freshly churned Irish butter and then Jordan saw her, spied her from across the grand ballroom where a few couples were waltzing to The Blue Danube being played by the small ensemble, and guests hovered in small circles chatting in the manner the privileged do. It was Evangeline Beauregard, the cosmetics billionaire from Atlanta. She had just crossed into the billionaire range with a new line of foundation products simply named "Women Only." At only thirty years old she was the world's youngest female billionaire. Jordan had read that her team of crack scientists, with the help of artificial intelligence, had developed a line of make-up products that sensed and detected hormonal levels on the recipient and if male hormones were detected the product broke apart and was rendered useless. Some news pundits labeled it the anti-drag queen defense. It was Evangeline's contribution to what she discreetly called the cause. And she had been rightly motivated to support the cause. Her first and only marriage so far, fell apart only months after being consummated when a flight she was taking to Asia was postponed to the next morning due to inclement weather, and she arrived unexpected back at home only to find her brand new groom on his knees in one of the pantries, gobbling down one of the hot, grubby landscapers who was cheated his ejaculation just as she waltzed into the kitchen. She had never seen a penis go limp in three seconds. It was a scandal she refused to take sitting down, hence her new line of no homo skin products. Jordan eyed her now, and couldn't help but be a little envious - she had three discreet security men, and they all looked like they had jumped off the latest issue of Gentlemen's Quarterly. To say she looked stunning tonight actually would be a disservice to the billionaire. She looked like someone who dropped out of a love story fairy tale, and the $40,000 Valentino Garavani Tulle Flora gown certainly helped. The designer had altered the original design to lower the breasts section and use gold and diamond encrusted shoulder straps in place of the original long sleeves. The tops of her breasts were magnificent - two mounds of pure cocoa satin with the nipples coquettishly peeking out from behind the translucent fabric. And when you are that wealthy you can do what she did: wear Miu Miu's sequined silk underwear and allow them to gently sparkle beneath the dress. Even Jordan thought she might be able to turn him straight in the right setting and alcohol content. Obviously, all eyes were on Evangeline now, with most using their cultured training by trying to not look like they were looking at her. Such tricks included but were not limited to pointing out a nearby painting to a companion, pointing at it but looking at the real subject of conversation, or glancing to the left or the right of the subject, as if looking for someone. But Cooper McNally didn't use any of those tricks because he wasn't cultured enough to be aware of them, and he really didn't care anyway. All he knew was what he was staring at was the most beautiful woman he had ever seen in his life. But he didn't even entertain any thoughts of what it would be like to actually meet her, to talk to her because he knew that he was so far down on the totem pole that it was the part that was pounded into the ground with mud caked around it. Now, glancing back at his so-called security detail Jordan became irritated but was limited in how he could react. He tried throwing an evil eye at the former tow driver, but Cooper's eyes seemed permanently locked in place. Then, the oddest thing happened. Evangeline took notice of Jordan and actually started walking towards him. He had briefly met her at a conference last year, and did not expect anyone of her caliber to remember him, but she apparently did. She arrived to him with her three security detail in the background, near Cooper. She extended a hand and Jordan nervously kissed it.

"It's Jordan, right?" she said.

"Yes ma'am. Jordan Sam.Thank you for remembering."

"Absolutely," she cooed. "We appreciate all that you do."

"I can't tell you how much pleasure it gives me to be at the ground roots of the cause," replied Jordan, almost pinching himself to make sure he wasn't dreaming. Now it seemed other guests weren't even trying to hide that they were observing the couple, not unlike a drama scene in a Broadway play. As he kept nervously rattling like a schoolboy who had just met his centerfold dream, Evangeline had already filtered him out with one of her classic pasted smiles still across her ethereal face. She was looking at Cooper McNalley, standing there in his private detail black suit and large black dress shoes. The package the security man was half-way trying to keep tucked behind his sleek dress pants, didn't fool the billionairess. She looked at the feet, the hands and the towering 6'4 height of the man and instinctively knew he wasn't swinging an average sized ding dong. And even being the very wealthy woman that she was, that was her terminology: *ding dong*. It came from her Georgia farmland roots where her grandmother used it and her mother wasn't the least bit shy to inject it into everyday conversation. She would say things like "He's probably a drunkard because he's got a little bitty ding dong," or "I swear, that man's ding dong was as big as a baseball bat." Anyway, there was something about Cooper's emerald greens, that reflected a downhome innocence and reminded her of her younger days on pawpaw's farm, that drew her attention to Jordan's security man. And then she had a brilliant idea and immediately pitched it to the lobbyist.

"I absolutely admire the posture of your security man," she whispered.

"How do you mean?" replied Jordan.

"His stance," she continued. "The way he stands there with his hands neatly folded in front and blends in with the crowd. I like the way his eyes gently scan the premises. Look - now - just look at my guy on the left. See how his eyes are darting back and forth. I don't like that. It's too obvious what he is doing. I will have my staff coach him later. But, listen. It's not him I am so concerned about. It's my guy in the middle. See the one with the red hair?"

"Yes," replied Jordan, taking note of the handsome Irish-looking security man who was a tad shorter than Jordan.

"He and the other one - to the right of him. They are not getting along so well," she lied. "I understand from my staff we have a little in-fighting between them. My personal assistant at home calls it a pissing contest."

"Hmmm," said Jordan. "Sort of an alpha male showdown, possibly vying for your attention?"

"Exactly," replied Evangeline. "And I must put an end to it - and guess what? You can help."

"Me?" said Jordan. "How?"

"By exchanging a security man with me."

"Huh?" said Jordan, confused but starting to hear what she was suggesting.

"What's your guy's name?" she continued.

"It's Cooper. Cooper McNally, but-"

"- I like the name. I do," said Evangeline. "The redhead is named Jack. Jack McDougal. He is really a nice, very nice man from what I know of him. Also polite, always yes ma'am this and yes ma'am that. He almost trips over himself to open doors for me. He's actually from Ireland - immigrated here about five years ago I am told. A single man but I have heard a few ladies have their eyes on him - including one of my housekeepers, but that's another story. So. An equal exchange? What do you say?"

"A what?" replied Jordan.

Evangeline snickered. "You are *the* Jordan Sam, right? The man behind Jordan Sam Group, one of the most influential lobbyist groups in the country?"

"Of course," laughed Jordan, his mind racing like a cougar, trying to think faster on his feet but feeling trapped nonetheless. This billionaire temptress is trying to take my man. What should I do? What should I say? I can't say, no, Evangeline. He's not really my security detail - he's my lover. He is the man of my dreams. *He's got 14 inches I can't live without?* She's got me trapped and I don't see a way out.

"Do your security men, like, live at your house," ventured Jordan, hoping maybe it was a job Cooper could come home from after his shifts. And what do I do with this Jack? I don't even really have a security detail and do not need one.

Now Evangeline laughed and gently slapped her knee. "Darling, I don't live in a *house*."

"Beg pardon. What do you live in?" asked Jordan, embarrassed that he did not know.

"In a castle outside of Atlanta," she replied. "To answer your question, yes, my security detail have very nice quarters on the castle grounds. I expect them to be on call 24 hours a day. As you can imagine, plenty of unexpected things arise. Last minute drop ins from international dignitaries. Gushing fashion designers flying in from Milan or Paris and then last minute call my staff to schedule a helicopter landing because they just want to "chill" with Evangeline and show her their latest designs. And let me tell you, if any one of them brings me another dress with five pink comforters flowing down one side and ten feet onto the floor, I will scream, Jordan, absolutely scream!"

And then Jordan realized he couldn't speak. He didn't have a reply, did not have a rebuttal, did not have a 'no Evangeline, I can't exchange my security man for your Jack.' He had nothing. Then he decided to take a huge chance. Stop thinking about it and just say it queer, he said to himself.

"It's Cooper's birthday at midnight," said Jordan. "I'm sorry, Evangeline. I can't let him go right now - I mean, let him leave my employment but," and then the lobbyist leaned in and whispered, "but he could, like, disappear for a few hours tonight if you get my drift. I think I will survive without his guard ship for a little bit."

And then the pasted smile of the billionairess turned into a smile so wide and brilliantly white Cooper almost pulled out his shades.

"I like you, Jor. You think fast on your feet. I'm going to share a secret. It won't surprise you that someone of my means knows a lot more than the average person. Let's just say I know your Stay In legislation comes - and how should I put this delicately- comes straight from *your* heart. Let's just leave it at that. But, now the good stuff. Yes, I appreciate your offering and you can ask Cooper to discreetly visit me upstairs, say, in about an hour. I will call off my dogs so he won't be stopped or questioned."

"Cool," replied Jordan. "I appreciate it. He'll love his Birthday present. Which room number shall I tell him?"

Evangeline laughed. "The entire top floor," she replied. I will make sure my elevator attendant allows him passage to the top. When the door opens he will be in my penthouse. Goodnight, Jor."

Jordan was practically swooning. She called me Jor. I guess that's my new moniker. Then the lobbyist waved Cooper over.

"I have another Birthday present for you, sir."

"Really? I mean the Jeep blew me away. I'm still pinching myself to make sure it's real, " said Cooper.

"Well get ready to really pinch yourself," chuckled Jordan. "You know the woman I was speaking with? That's Evangeline Beauregard. She's a cosmetics billionaire. Anyway, she and I chatted about you. Happy Birthday."

"Huh?" said Cooper.

"In about an hour navigate back to the lobby and see the penthouse elevator attendant. He will be expecting you," replied the lobbyist.

"What do I do when I get there?" said Cooper, still puzzled.

"Why take the elevator to the top and you'll see Evangeline when you get off. Then you pick her up and carry her to the bed and show her how much of a man you are."

Jordan looked at Cooper's eyes as he realized what his Birthday present was. Then the lobbyist's eyes were directed to the pelvic region of his man. Oh no, he thought.

Cooper saw him looking and then he too looked down at himself. Unable to stop it, his tool was rising up at an alarming rate.

"Find a chair, Coop. Hurry," said Jordan."

"I'm sorry, " apologized Coop. "After what you just told me it's about to be tent city in this fancy new hotel."

Chapter Six

When the elevator door to the penthouse opened, Cooper McNally found himself faced with a Goddess of proportions the likes he had never even imagined in his younger rub one off days. As she stood there in a floor length Kiki De Montparnass negligee, she radiated a beauty that seemed almost unattainable - was unattainable to the average man. Her thick blond mane showered down past her petite shoulders, a cascade of long locks and radiance. A living, breathing female hourglass Cooper thought he could see the sexual heat permeating off her, like the translucent waves of an August French Quarter, visible to the eye, consuming your every pore, inviting you to shed man made fabrics designed to hide the body from others and to say the hell with it, live man, live.

"Hey," he managed to say gruffly, his masculinity now projecting from the red-alert level of testosterone of his muscular, 6 '4 body.

She motioned feather-like with her lithe arm, indicating a recliner in the auditorium-sized open spaced suite with wall to ceiling glass bringing the mighty Mississippi River right into the room. He somehow managed to walk over to the chair and sit down while Evangeline poured him a whiskey neat. When you are in her wealth range you don't ask silly questions like what do you want to drink. Your money and power already know what the guest should drink - that's why you are a billionaire. You could read the face of a Benedictine monk.

"It's your birthday in a few minutes," she said.

"Yes ma'am," replied Cooper.

"No formalities here," she chuckled. "Guzzle that whiskey down like a man and be a good boy and come here and undo my negligee."

Cooper downed the drink and almost trembling, he got up from the recliner. He was nervous because he had never hit a woman as fine as Evangeline - not one even close to her caliber. As he reached her she continued.

"Let me take off your shirt first. Take off your jacket."

Cooper took off his suit jacket and tossed it on a sofa. Then Evangeline began slowly unbuttoning his shirt, running her smooth hands across his chest, caressing his biceps. Now she buried her face in his thick mat of chest hair and breathed in. She nuzzled his underarm, a waft of sweet man sweat tinged with Tom's Alpine Sage underarm deodorant. Then she reached down and unbuckled his belt and Cooper's already semi-hard plantain began to rise up even more. Evageline then lowered to her knees and unlatched his dress pants and using her teeth began to unzip Cooper. She slowly pulled down his pants and then she was faced with his boxer shorts and a canopy the size of which she had never seen. She began to murmur as she slowly pulled down his boxers and then gasped as he was released in her face, his giant-ness soaring half way up his washboard belly, so much larger than she even imagined. Now she put her soft, glossed lips on the head and moved her long tongue around and around, causing Cooper's machismo baton to throb and jerk, to the point she had to take hold of it with both hands to calm it down. *It was as if it had a brain all its own.*

"Kick off your shoes," she pleaded, and he did, wildly, with abandon and then she pulled his pants and boxers all the way down and he knew to step out of them. Now his towering, masculine body stood before her, ready to give her his gift and she put his hands on her negligee, signaling to remove it and he fumbled with the zipper and began kissing her shoulders as he did. He pulled down her $2,000 sequined panties and now had her naked and she looked up at him.

"Take me to the bed."

No better words ever spoke, thought the wrecker driver and he picked her up and walked over to the bed across the room and gently lowered her onto it. Now he slowly leaned over her, his tool pointing straight out in anticipation of taking her. She put her arms around him and pulled him closer to her. Cooper began kissing her passionately, pushing his tongue deep into her mouth, moaning, lowering his head onto her titties and taking her large cocoa nipples in his mouth, licking her as she took hold of him and tried to guide him in. Cooper had to rise up over a foot so she could aim his head. Now he was partially in and knew from experience he would need to slowly allow himself to find the sweet spot, to be gentle and yet aggressive, to show his masculinity and that he was worthy of this present. As he got in deeper Evangeline moaned and dug her nails into his back.

"Go…all…all…in…" she moaned and Cooper humped in more, beginning to find the right rhythm, gyrating in and out, way up and then further down, up to the head almost coming out but not, and then in, further in as she clung to him and felt the full manhood of Cooper deep inside her. They were one now and sensed he should increase his motion and he did. He was pumping up and down faster and feeling the beginnings of a surge he knew would be the most incredible ever. He opened his eyes and looked at the beauty clinging beneath him, the sheer radiance of this woman who wanted him, wanted Cooper McNally, a plain ole tow truck driver to take her and bring her to that trip fantastic. And a trip fantastic it was. He could feel her juices and sense that point where she would feel his giant mushroom head hit the spot that would set off her cataclysmic eruption and he was determined to share that with her so sweating and panting he was all the way in her and then stopped and said gruffly "Don't move babe," and she remained still so he would not erupt in her before she was ready. Now he started the motion again and Evangeline felt herself priming up to the moment, excited by the man who was a lover the likes she had never experienced. He knew how to take her, to enter her, to penetrate ever so slowly at first and then increase his rhythm with her in mind, to caress her and yet mount over her like the six foot four, hundred percent wild sex man he was, using what he had with a talent unmatched, unparalleled. Now she felt herself surging up and dug her nails into his back further so he would know and he moaned, crying out in a guttural manliness, he was about to bring it to her and it would be a prize so abundant she would not stop coming and then she screamed - a raw, primitive woman scream that had not one note of fear or pain but rather a voice from the beginning of humankind, a visceral pleasure expression for all women, from then and now, a purity that could not be expressed in words nor any art.

"Aaaaaaaaaaaaahhhhhhhhhhhhhhhhhhh!
Aaaaaaaaaaaaaaaaaaaahhhhhhhhhhhhhhhhhhhh
Cooooopperrrrr!"

Now she knew one of the primary reasons for existence, and a reward so precious it made her cry. The joy tears sprung from her eyes as she bucked with Cooper and they rocketed together to a place that was blowing their collective mind. Cooper hollered so loud it filled the room with the sense of an undiscovered jungle, a place not even on the map, and had other animals been present they would have paused in awe.

Ooh! Ooohhh! Ahhhh! Oooooooooooooooooooooooo
Ahhhhhh! Damn! Damn! Damn!!! Ahhhhhhhh!"

 They writhed and then rolled, one over the other and still
clinging to each other as if this were how they should have
been born, this was how they should live every day. Bathed in
their collective, sweet sweat they melded into one creation of
indescribable pleasure and with her Cooper kept giving, kept
rocketing it inside her so intensely she realized at that very
moment she had never felt such pleasure. He couldn't stop
giving it to her, didn't want to stop, pumped her hard now at
hummingbird pace. The rocket had reached outer space. Now
they knew the real meaning of life.

When they were both spent he gently exited her and slowly
rolled to his side, she still in his arms, his face in her breasts,
her tousled hair on his hairy chest. And this is how they
almost instantly fell to sleep because one cannot stay awake
after such pleasure, such primitive beauty. Even if they could,
what would they say? *Nothing. Because there are no words.
None.*

At almost 3:00 AM in the ballroom of Le Arrondissement Hotel, the crowd had dramatically thinned. Only those who were having a hard time ending the fun, and their designated drivers, remained. Staff in white jackets moved about silently and cleared tables, the clinking of glass and silverware now in place of the earlier merriment. Jordan Sam was beside himself with anxiety. He had already been politely thwarted by the penthouse private elevator attendant. "No sir," he smiled brightly. Only preapproved guests, he was instructed. But they've been up there for three hours, protested Jordan, a statement met with silence because of privacy concerns and something best left to the imagination. There was nothing else to do but get a room and stay the rest of the night. The front desk attendant informed him with a smile and attitude so happy he might have been informing the guest that he had just won the lottery. "There are no rooms, sir. The hotel has been booked to capacity for several months now."

"But do you know who I am?" protested Jordan?" I am the man behind Stay In. I am a multimillionaire."

Now the desk clerk laughed. He couldn't hold back any longer.

"Sir, I appreciate your…status - I really do, but FYI - every guest in this hotel is a millionaire or even a billionaire. Millionaire? Join the crowd," he chuckled politely." Then the attendant looked at a computer screen.

"I checked and there are rooms at the Motel 6 which is about a mile down the street. Shall I reserve a room for you?"

Jordan stormed out of the hotel and stood around at the valet park for what seemed like forever. Finally a valet appeared and retrieved Cooper's Jeep. On the way home Jordan found himself wanting to cry. I don't understand, he thought. I offered up Cooper for a toss in the hay and expected him back down to the party in no time. I mean how long would it take him to get off with the likes of Evangeleine? She's probably trying to steal him from me but good luck, I know Coop is true to me. I'm the one who took all of him first. I bought him a Jeep for his birthday. I allow him to live in my home and he doesn't even have to work! What else would he want? Once home Jordan tore off his clothes and just let them remain in a pile on the carpet. He crawled into bed and clutched the pillows, trying to fight back the tears but the tears had a mind of their own and out they came, squirting like a sprinkler jump-starting when first turned on - sputtering, spurting and then swoosh, out sprays the water and those were his tears tonight as he imagined the worst, considered that his man may have been stolen with his very help. *Here Evangeline, take my man, Yeah, let him ride up your private elevator and jump in your billionairess bed. I'm not just giving you 10 or 12 inches of him: take all 14, and maybe you can squeeze another inch out of him. Take him and if you like it you can keep him!*

It was around 8:00 AM when Jordan, laying in a disarray of pillows, sheets and blankets, woke to the sound of someone walking into his bedroom.

"It's just me, babe," Cooper said gently.

Jordan stretched his arms over his head and yawned, bent like a pretzel and then throwing his long legs up in the air bounced up and sat on the edge of the bed. He rubbed his eyes with his knuckles and then blinked twice because Cooper was wearing a pair of Brunello Cucinell Celeste blue cashmere sweatpants that he knew to cost $3,500 because he himself almost bought

a pair but yielded to the sticker shock and bought the $900.00
Cotton French Terry instead.

"Are those her birthday gift to you?" he inquired.

"You mean the sweats?" replied Cooper. "Yeah, she made a
call and before I knew it they were delivered to the room."
And then he pulled down the sweatpants.

"She also bought these boxers. Maybe I heard her wrong but I
think these cost around $400.00. She said they are
Ver-Say-See, I think?"

"Ver sach-chee," Jordan corrected him. Cooper pulled the
sweats back up and Jordan couldn't help but notice the outline
of his penis snaking down his leg, past his thigh.

"I'm not sure about the coupling of sweatpants with boxers,"
chuckled Jordan.

"Yeah, I thought about that too but Evang said I should be
proud of what I've got and if anyone doesn't like it they can -
how did she put it - they can look the other way," said Cooper.

"*Evang?*" replied Jordan.

"Yeah, she asked me to call her by her nickname. I mean, she called me Coop so what the hay," he said. Then he paused and almost hesitated.

"Hey, look Jordan. Look man, I appreciate all that you've done for me - I really do."

"But…" replied Jordan, sensing what was coming.

"But Evang - me and her - well, we really hit it off last night. I mean I can't even put into words - I mean it's hard to put into words what happened last night. It like, changed my world - turned it upside down," said Cooper.

"You like her because she has a lot more money than me," said Jordan.

"No, no, it ain't like that," said Cooper, walking towards Jordan. "I mean bro, you knew I was like straight, right? I mean I let you -"

" -Let me?" interrupted the lobbyist. "You didn't *let me* anything. I gave you - gave you the feeling you had never experienced. I took all of you mister and I mean all of you. I gave you my hot tea treatment and I have never done that for a man."

"Yeah, I know," replied Cooper, "and it felt great, it really did."

"I bought you a $55,000 Jeep for your Birthday," continued Jordan.

"And I appreciate it," said Cooper. "Umm, come here, walk over to the window."

Jordan got up and looked out the window at the drive way.

"Is that what I think it is?" he said incredulously.

"A Bugatti," nodded Cooper. "It's the La Voiture Noire, or something like that. She made me practice saying it."

"So she is lending you a 19 million dollar car," said Jordan. "That's crazy."

Cooper frowned. "Not lend."

"Not lend?" cried Jordan, his voice rising to a fever pitch.
"She bought you a 19 million dollar car in the middle of the
night?"

"No, this morning," said Cooper. It was like the sweatpants.
She made one call and then an hour later it was in the valet
park. I couldn't believe it myself. Hey man, I'm sorry - and
look, I understand I shouldn't keep the Jeep so you can take it
back, right. So it's not so bad afterall," said Cooper.

"Not so bad afterall?" cried Jordan. "I loved you. And that car
outside is worth more than my bank account."

" That's what she said, but wow, okay," said Cooper. "Yeah, I
get it but like I said, I'm straight."

"You weren't so straight when I was down between your legs
warming your zucchini with hot chamomile tea! Get out!
Leave please!"

Cooper walked slowly out of the room and then at the door turned around. "I do appreciate everything you did for me Jordan - I really do. You take care man. You'll find another guy. I know you will."

Then, as he was about to close the door he turned sound again. "Hey man, since you seem to like wrecker drivers, a bunch of them hang out after work at Larry's on Johnson Street. It's a little alley off Canal, a bar where they go and have beer and shoot the bull."

Chapter Seven

The breakup with Cooper McNally had a profound effect on Jordan Sam. The most frustrating thing about it was that he couldn't say a word about it. He couldn't cry to a friend or throw the traditional public temper tantrum straight and openly gay people get to throw. No, he chose to stay in, to keep his gay shenanigans to himself. About a week after the break up with Cooper, Jordan was asked to be the keynote speaker at a special luncheon organized by the National Anti-DEI League. The passage of laws in at least 22 states had provided a momentum the group so desperately wanted and their goal now was to have federal legislation implemented, laws that would prohibit any federal funding to schools and other institutions that catered to the Diversity, Equality, Inclusion mindset. It took Jordan over three hours to write the speech but the day of the event arrived and he was introduced to an audience of over 500 key members, by the president of the League.

"Gentlemen - and take note I begin with Gentlemen and do not include the word Ladies because as we all know this is not needed. Right?! Gentlemen, it gives me great pleasure to introduce a man who really does not need much of an introduction. Jordan Sam is a household name in our world. His firm, the Jordan Sam Group is synonymous with American family tradition, with save the family, with keep our families and children safe from evil forces that threaten us every day of our lives. The mastermind behind legislation now pending full congressional approval and a signature by the President of the United States, Jordan Sam's *Stay in* is a testament to the progress we have achieved. For the first time in history homosexuals who choose to flaunt their lifestyle in public, could be prosecuted under federal law. Many of our states already have similar legislation in place. Jordan helped us to say enough is enough: we know you are out there gay folks, and we are not trying to wipe you from existence. We only want you to respect our children, respect our classrooms and keep your dang homosexuality to yourselves! Now Jordan is coordinating another major movement - ours, the Anti-DEI League. For too long, states and the federal government have funded schools including colleges and universities for programs that seek to provide preferences to minorities and homosexuals in hiring practices and a number of social environments. These people should not be receiving our hard earned tax dollars to promote their agendas. Without further ado, I give you Jordan Sam!"

Jordan tried to walk as masculine as he could to the podium, and even discreetly scratched his balls just a little bit, to show his manliness. Now he looked out at the crowd and began his speech.

"D-E-I," he began rather loudly. "Disturbed Elevated Individuals. That's what I call them. People who because of the color of their skin, because of their race or creed, because of their sexual preference, think the government owes them money to help them cheat in order to get a job, to help them skip the line and go all the way to the front where they want special treatment because awe, they were dealt a bad card in life and people aren't treating them fairly. We say no to this funding so you can take your sour grapes and make a little gay salad with it out of your own pocket!"

The crowd broke into tumultuous applause. Jordan was hot, was on a roll this afternoon.

"White hetrosexuals founded this great country of ours! There, I said it. I addressed the elephant in the room. We are not afraid of the truth. We will not back down from our White heritage. The fact of the matter is we are the leaders of this country. We are the people who almost 250 years ago kindly negotiated with the Indians and took control of this land, and with hard work and lots of sweat we made it great. Now the minorities and homosexuals want to take all of that from us. They want to take credit for what we've done and - get this: they want the government to help them by allowing them to skip the line of hard work and prayer and go to the front of the line in the job place and schools. Like a great leader before me said so eloquently: Read My Lips. But this time we are saying No Diversity. No Equality. No Inclusion. Things will remain as they are because this is our land and you people - you people should be happy, should be jumping up and down with joy that we allow you to live amongst us and work, attend school, live good lives. But we've got one thing to tell you mister: *We run this show. Us.* You are not for a moment going to infiltrate our ranks. No sir! Not an inch!"

Unless you've got 14 inches and in that case I will get back with you.

Now the crowd stood in unison and deafening applause filled the ears of the lobbyist. They asked, and he delivered because that's what he did. Now the president of the League took back the stage.

"What did I tell you!" he cried. "What I don't know is why I haven't seen any Jordan Sam for President signs in yards across this great nation!" The crowd broke into applause again. "Does anyone have any questions? Grab your chance while we have Jordan here. A woman in the audience raised her hand.

"Yes ma'am," said the president.

"Thank you," she began. "This question is for Jordan. We've seen in the news off and on over the past few years allegations by some politicians and news media that you are a closet gay. They point out that in your mid-Sixties you have never been married, and, and, well, to state the obvious you do have um, a few feminine mannerisms - not that that is bad. Don't get me wrong. I'm only paraphrasing what the media has said."

Now that was dead silence in the banquet room. Even the servers stopped in their duties and it seemed all eyes were on the lobbyist. Jordan was smiling but behind his smile he was petrified. Not that he hadn't been asked the question before, it was just now, with this large audience, the questions spooked him. Then he had a rare epiphany. He would run with it.

"Well, thank you for the question. It's one that has been presented to me before and I don't mind in the least answering it. But first, I want to point out that you said 'closet gay.' So, even if I were closet gay isn't this the very thing we are striving for - for all openly gay homosexuals to go back in the closet, that we don't mind their existence but what we do strongly mind is them flaunting their gayness to the world. If I were gay then I should be the poster boy for Stay In, right? What better person to promote the legislation than the very type of person for whom it's meant. But having said that, the answer to your question is no, *I am not gay and have never been gay.* Yes, I do have some mannerisms some people could interpret as feminine, and therefore homosexual. I would also like to point out that not all homosexuals are feminine - and that's part of the problem we face - all these chameleon type gays running around looking and acting hetrosexual, making it hard for us to identify them and make sure they are in compliance with our state and federal laws. Now, I'll end my answer with a question to all of you. *Do any of you know any*

*beautiful, wealthy cougars out there because Jordan Sam is
on the prowl!"*

Laughter fills the room coupled with a standing ovation of
applause and knee-slapping. Once again Jordan Sam had won
his audience. People could accuse him of being gay until they
were blue in the face. He did the world even one better than
Stay In. He was the inventor of the next stage of the process:
Self Deny. One day after the pending bills have passed he will
wow his clients and America with an even better solution:
staying in the closet will not be enough anymore. Be gay but
don't be gay. Live in a deep closet of gayness but you are not
really gay. One day he dreamed of Wikipedia and the major
dictionaries doing something so phenomenal the whole world
would look at the inventor behind it - Jordan Sam - and
admire him with all their might: remove the word gay from
existence. Delete it. It doesn't exist. There's nothing to discuss
because there is no gay. *Be gone with you gay. Be gone.*

To celebrate his success at the Anti-DEI League luncheon
Jordan got a wild hair up his ass and, also feeling lonely with
Cooper out of his life, decided to take Coop's advice and
check out the bar where he said a lot of tow drivers hung out
after work. He found a parking garage near Larry's bar and

dressed in a new tan casual light cotton sports suit he opened the door leading into the bar. It was so dark inside he had to stand at the entrance for a moment to adjust to it. Then he spied the long bar straight ahead, lined with what appeared to be working class men in various uniforms - navy blue pants and matching shirts with embroidered names on the pockets, some men in fluorescent green vests and dark work pants. They were all talking loudly, drinking from frosted beer mugs and bottles, a row of large screens plastered on the wall behind the two bartenders. Whiskey Glasses by Morgan Wallen played loudly over the sound system.

"I'ma need some whiskey glasses
'Cause I don't wanna see the truth
She's probably making out on the couch right now
With someone new

Jordan walked up to the bar and ordered a scotch neat. The bartender gave him a second look because he didn't seem to fit in, but he wasn't the first to pop in and not meld with the usual crowd. A few of the men glanced over while they shot the bull with the others, perhaps thinking the same thing, but life went on and Jordan has passed the first hurdle - just getting in the bar and getting a drink with no road bumps. As he glanced across the bar he noticed several good-looking masculine men he wouldn't mind meeting. There was something about wrecker drivers that intrigued him, and it seemed like most of them were eye candy and very masculine. Then he saw a young guy sitting at the other end of the bar. He stood out because he was by himself, smoking a cigarette and seemed to be lost in thought. But even from across the bar Jordan could see he was a looker: medium height, not skinny but not fat, short black crew-cut style haircut and a classic masculine face: sort of squared and with a nice long nose and just the right size ears to fit his face. He had on a blue work uniform and Cooper could see the white embroidered pocket but was too far to read it. Now he saw that the man's beer stein was empty and he was talking to the bartender and looking in his wallet, rummaging through his front pockets but didn't seem to produce any money for another beer. When the bartender turned away from the man he looked in Jordan's direction and feeling this was the time to make his move. Jordan waved him over.

"I'll have another scotch," said Jordan. "And give that man at the other end a beer. Looks like he couldn't find his money."

The bartender frowned, but it wasn't like he hadn't seen a
fruit wander in here before. He gave Jordan his drink and then
delivered a fresh one to the man at the other end, and nodded
in Jordan's direction. The man looked and then raised his beer
mug to Jordan. There was an empty barstool next to Jordan so
he pointed at it and the man picked up his beer and walked
over. He had a masculine gait and as he got closer Jordan
could read his name patch: Genovese Towing and below that:
Antonio Giuseppe. Hmm, thought Jordan as the man sat next
to him. Italian.

"Thanks for the beer man," said Antonio. "I guess you saw
me fumbling for some cash. Antonio. Antonio Giuseppe.
What's your name," he said, extending a grease stained,
callous hand. He was in his early Forties and his hands had
the look of a man who had always worked with them.

"I'm Jordan Sam. Pleased to meet you." Jordan spoke with a
bit more femininity than he would at a conference or in other
public places. The man raised his eyebrows and it seemed he
was a quick study. In his business he must have come across a
few he had to tow.

"I guess you can see from my shirt I was a wrecker driver. What do you do?" asked Antonio.

"I'm a political consultant," said Jordan, not wanting to provide much detail.

"Nice," nodded Antonio.

"You said you *were* a wrecker driver," said Jordan.

"Yeah,"replied Antonio. "I got fired today."

"Oh, wow. Sorry to hear that," said Jordan.

"Yeah, scratched up a lady's car with the winch. Even though the company insurance is paying for the repaint they still let me go. Well, to be honest, it happened another time, last year."

"Gotcha," said Jordan. "Have you ever done any mechanic work?"

"Heck yeah," replied Antonio. "I sometimes still do that on the side, but since I mostly got out of it when I started wrecking, it's been slow. Why, you know somebody need'in some work?"

"If you can tune up a Jaguar then yes, me," said Jordan.

"Shoot, yeah I can do that," said Antonio, sliding his stool a little closer to Jordan. "I might have to find a garage I can use-"

"That won't be necessary," said Jordan. I have a three bay garage at my house and one of the bay's is equipped with a lift and a big old red tool box I confess I have never opened," Jordan slapped his knee and slid into a deep feminine side of himself.

"Nice," said Antonio, studying the strange man. "When you want me to stop by?"

"Tonight," replied Jordan, killing the rest of the scotch in his glass and motioning to the bartender for another one and a beer for the former tow driver.

"Nice," replied Antonio, adding, "I been dating this gal you know. But it's nothing serious right now." Then he leaned in and said in a lower voice, "I think it's because I'm too big, if you get my drift," and he winked.

Jordan twirled on his barstool and looked Antonio up and down and then his eyes stopped on his large black work boots. "Dang, you have big feet. What size?"

"16," said Antonio, proudly. "You think that's big."

Was that a question or a statement? Jordan couldn't tell but it sounded like 'you think *that's* big.' Suddenly Antonio stood up.

"Just need to stretch,"he said, and Jordan's eyes riveted to his pants zipper and it seemed to him there was a lot of material down there.

"Did I tell you I'm Italian?" asked Antonio.

"No," said Jordan, "but I could tell from your name."

"Well, you know what they say about Italian men, right?"

Is he going where I think he's going, thought Jordan, deciding to play dumb. "No, what do they say?"

And then Antonio grinned and grabbed hold of himself and held his grip there for a few seconds.

"Oh," said Jordan. "You know what, yeah, I've heard that. Well, you want to follow me to my house? It's not far. I'll park in the repair bay and you can take a look at it. You don't have to do the whole tune-up tonight."

"Sure," said Antonio, and they walked out of the bar.

The former tow driver followed Jordan in his old white Ford pick-up truck with a souped up muffler that added to his machismo, and Jordan couldn't wait until he was in the garage and then walk out to "check up on things." He's got size 16 feet. He's Italian and he has a girlfriend who is afraid of what he's hanging below the belt. Could it be possible I have hit another home run? I mean I wouldn't expect him to be another Cooper McNally, but if he's at least a foot long that will be wonderful. And won't he be surprised when I take that like it's an appetizer and I'm waiting on the entree.

After Antonio oohed and ahhed about the size of the house he went back in the garage, found a brand new runner hanging on a wall and slid under the car. Jordan went inside and changed into something more feminine, sprayed on some girly smelling cologne, made two drinks and mosied out to the garage. He looked at Antonio laying on his back, his legs apart looking so manly, and couldn't wait to see what was underneath those greasy, sweaty work pants.

"Come on up sir," said Jordan. "I made you a whiskey."

Antonio slid out and lifted himself up, standing next to the car with the front of his pants bunched up from laying down. He lowered his hand and adjusted himself, looking at Jordan who was watching. The mechanic downed his whiskey and then moved closer to the lobbyist.

"Why don't you drop down in front of this Italian stallion and lick his big hairy nuts," he ordered.

Jordan didn't need any additional instruction and quickly laid down his drink. Nervous and excited he unbuckled the mechanic's belt, unsnapped his pants and pulled them down a little past his thighs. Now he was faced with his white boxer shorts and a tent of a sort poking out. But it was the "of a sort' part that immediately disturbed the lobbyist. He had expected to see a Barnum and Bailey monstrosity ballooning out - something like Cooper but maybe not exactly that large. Hesitantly, and now nervous for a different reason he reached inside the fly of the boxers and found the erect mechanic. His hand froze, and was unable to move. Antonio looked down on him and said, "You ok?"

"Uh, yes. Of course," replied Jordan, lying. Now he extracted the tool and it came out of the opening easily. That was because at about 8 inches it was like taking a piece of candy from a baby. Jordan was panicking inside. He said it was big, said the girl he is dating is afraid of it *because it's so big*. This was like going to the ballpark, asking for the large hotdog and instead of the footlong they give you the six inch weenie, or getting a Gherkin instead of a dill.

"Now I will tell you what I told the gal," said Antonio. "Don't be scared of it. Just take a little at a time. It takes practice and I will work with you. Patience is my middle name."

Yeah, and your first name is Pee Wee Tater Tot, thought
Jordan.

What the heck. He's here. Might as well make the best of it,
so he moved his head down on the mechanic and in one fell
swoop he had the whole thing inside and was using his tongue
to lick his boys - and then he put those in his mouth too. It
was like going to one of those restaurants where the chef is a
minimalist and the server brings a huge plate to the table with
a piece of steak the size of a half dollar.

"Whoa!" moaned Antonio as Jordan grabbed him from behind
and tried to get him in further, and then remembered there was
no further. With additional prompting Jordan conveyed that it
was okay to pretend he was on a wild bull at the rodeo and in
a few minutes Antonio hollered so loud one of the hooks on
an MDF board fell off and clinked onto the concrete floor.
Pulling up his pants he whistled and said "You sure know
what you are doing. You should be in the movies - the good
kind of movies."

Jordan thanked him and thought, *you should be in an*
urologist's office - the kind where you get your rod stretched.
"You know what?" said Jordan. "I just remembered that if I let

anyone but an authorized shop work on this car, it voids the warranty." He reached in his wallet and took out a hundred dollar bill. "But you came over here so I still owe you. Here you go. And oh, I am getting a migraine. I'm not trying to give you the bum's rush…"

Chapter Eight

Speaking of bum's rush, thought Jordan Sam as he made notes for his next ethereal legislation package to present on behalf of his clients saving America from men who like men, women who like women, and those who dare claim God got it wrong when he assigned them mentally right but anatomically wrong, those damn rainbow flags need a major bum's rush. Although he wished there was a way to stop people from flying them at their homes and private businesses, he was resigned to accepting he could only help the public sector. Public schools were the big prize because they are tax-payer funded. Several states had already banned the flags at schools so now the aim was to make it a federal law.

Lower the Rainbow would be the prize codification he would complete and present to his esteemed clients. It would be the de facto argument against gay rainbow flags on any public property in America. Jordan hoped that it would catch on in the private sector as well. As he produced his foundation notes for the law, he lifted his head up from his keyboard as he composed one of the shining lines of the law. At this moment he felt so proud of himself. He knew it would be the single, most important line that people remember. He actually stopped after he wrote the sentence, raised his right hand and patted the left upper part of his back. That's right, he thought. *This is so good I deserve a self-pat on the back.*

The only rainbows there should be, are the rainbow's in the sky. The ones where we imagine a pot of gold at the end. For homosexuals to steal this from us is unconscionable.

"Oh my God," he said out loud. This deserves a night on the town. Yes, I will find a man, but I will do it without cutting down a single tree. I will do it from deep inside my own little world, not disturbing any others. But what about all the other men and women who like me are good citizens and remain in the closet? Who is standing up for them? I am, but I could do even better. But mother needs sustenance and not just any sustenance. I need a wooly mammoth. Jordan went to work online and frantically researched the subject. Very soon it became clear it was time for an international vacation. He now knew he would have to visit an iconic country in South America. He knew he would have to fly to Ecuador where it is

said the most endowed men in the world live. No man has less
than 7 there, and most have much, much more. He needed to
go now, to appease his hunger and so he arranged for a flight
the very next day. By the end of the day he had landed in
Quito and got on a connecting flight to the largest city,
Guayaquil, and then a little hopper to Playas where he
checked into the Grand Playas Real. His logic for coming to
the beach town was the men would be in swim trunks, half
naked already, providing him better scoping capabilities. He
didn't have to wait long to see some of the goods. He took a
light snack in his room and then walked out to the beach
below just a little after sunset. It was a romantic beach with
couples holding hands, stooping for seashells, embracing and
kissing as night fell in the South America beach town. He
walked along the beach and soon found what appeared to be a
surfer's bar, El Tablista, on the edge of the water. He decided
to walk up and order a beer. There was a sizable crowd of
shirtless men shooting the bull with one another, and Jordan
ordered what they were all drinking - Cerveceria Nacional. He
had only been there for a few minutes when he noticed that
nearly all the men he observed looked like they had shoplifted
zucchinis and stuffed them down their pants. This was a good
sign - not here for even a few hours and the first place he
visits is delivering the goods. As he sipped his beer it

suddenly occurred to him he didn't see any surfboards and he didn't see any woman. And then he saw something that caused him to almost drop his bottle of beer: two men embracing. Now a young, tall Ecuadoran approached him. The way he walked indicated to Jordan that he was a member of the club. My God, he thought, I walked up to a pansy bar on the beach. I've got to get out of here. But the young man addressed him.

"Hi, you are American, no?"

"Yes," replied Jordan.

"I speak the English," replied the man, who had black hair and dark eyes, a flashy smile.

"Good," replied Jordan, thinking, *Why don't you go practice it on someone else?" I'm not into bumping cooch.*

"What you look for?" asked the man, getting straight to the point.

What the heck, thought Jordan. No one knows me here and I'm about to run from this sandcastle of miss things, so why not tell him.

"I am looking for the big one, on a straight hombre - straight, not gay. Big, real big - mucho grande."

The man's eyes widened. "Oh, yes, okay, yes, the big one but not the gay. Mucho grande. Yes." Then his face lit up. "Un momento, senor. Momento. Stay," he said excitedly and then ran behind the bar. When he came back a man holding a broom and weighing about 300 pounds was walking slowly behind him.

"I found the big one - Eduardo. He do the clean here at the bar. He no gay but he tell me the gay is good. He say he *want* the gay. The gay can have him now, *now* - room behind this bar. You want Eduardo?"

Jordan knew there was only one thing he could do. Now all the patrons in the bar stood up as Eduardo pointed at the gringo.

"I never see any man run on the sand that fast," he said.

"It's like he's on a racetrack," said another. "What," laughed
the man. ""Eduardo, did you flash your trompa de elefante at
him?"

Eduardo frowned and scratched his head. "I get no chance to
show him, or tell him I'm in that book."

Everyone laughed. The 300 pound cleaning man was so proud
of making it in the Guiness World Book of Records on behalf
of Ecuador. Most of them had gotten a peek at his claim to
fame, but they always made sure his pal was around to help,
because they didn't want the task of having to tug it out and
help hold it. It took two sets of hands to appreciate the breadth
and scope of his *pene de gigante.*

Back in his hotel room Jordan was still out of breath. What a
scare, he thought. And they think I didn't see that he had
apparently stuffed part of a broom stick down his pants, to
entice me. What next, he thought. Where should I go to find
Eldorado? And then a most magical thing happened: his
phone rang. He recognized Coop's number. His heart raced.

"Hello?", answered Jordan.

"Hey babe. It's the Coop."

And at that very moment Jordan was overwhelmed with emotion. Here he was in a foreign land, almost attacked by a big, straight janitor, and now the soothing, familiar voice of Cooper McNally drifts in from across the world.

"Coop? Oh Coop. How are you sir?" he almost cried.

"You okay, babe?" asked Cooper.

This almost brought Jordan to tears. His man cared, was asking about him. But then he remembered he wasn't his man anymore. He belonged to Evangeline.

"I'm in Ecuador," said Jordan. "I don't even know what I'm doing here." And then the lobbyist had a little nervous breakdown, sobbing, his words hiccuping out between dramatic intakes of breath.

"Oh babe, your man will take care of you. Evang is history. She dumped me for a rapper she met in L.A. She took back the Bugatti, handed me $5,000 and basically told me to hit the road. You still got that Jeep?"

Jordan laughed between sobs. "Mister, I will get that Jeep back, only one better."

"Come back home baby. Get on that plane now. Your man needs you by his side," said Cooper gruffly.

Jordan already started throwing stuff into his suitcase as he was talking. "I'm on the way, Coop. I don't know why I let you go the first time. I should have put up a fight for you."

"Yeah baby, fight for your man," said Cooper.

At the airport in Quito, Jordan was passing through security when the guard who was scanning him bumped up against his butt. The lobbyist turned and looked down at the guard. Then his jaw dropped. Stretched down in line with the guard's knee was the unmistakable outline of a monstrous tool. Jordan couldn't stop looking. It had to be at least 20 inches long. The guard chastised him.

"No look so long," he admonished. "If it grow here I lose my job."

When Jordan pulled into his driveway it was raining and he caught a glimpse of Cooper standing in the front entrance, drenched. He jumped out of his car and ran up to him and Cooper picked him up off his feet, hugging him, smothering him with wet, rainy kisses. They didn't even talk as they rushed inside and landed on the first sofa they found, Cooper on top of Jordan, pressing into him so tight it was almost as if they were one. The former wrecker driver was no longer shy about kissing either and planted a deep French style tongue into Jordan's waiting mouth, causing the lobbyist to moan, cry out in pleasure. They tore off their clothes and made love right there in the family room. Once they recovered, Cooper picked up Jordan in his arms and carried him to Jordan's bedroom where he crawled under the covers with him and they fell intertwined into a deep arms and legs pretzel sleep. When Coop woke the next morning there was a tray with English muffin, egg and ham, and a hot cup of coffee and glass of freshly squeezed orange juice.

"Baby, you spoiling me,: said Cooper, rubbing his eyes. "I could marry somebody like you."

Jordan stopped in his tracks and looked at Cooper.

"Really? Do you mean that?"

"Yes I mean that. I don't care if the whole world knows. So what, a man marries another man. Big deal. Anyway, the people who don't like it do not pay a penny of my bills. They mean nothing to me. Why should I live my life to please their expectations?"

"Coop…Coop…are you asking what I think you are?"

"Will you marry me Jordan Sam? To have and to hold, till death do us part?" said Cooper.

"Coop!" cried Jordan. "Yes! Yes I will!"

"But what about your business, and what you do for all those folks?" said Cooper.

"That's about to change," replied Jordan. "My mind is already racing on that subject. I am so stupid. This whole time I was against being myself because I was afraid of love and ashamed that I didn't have love. So I built a campaign against the ones who already have what I didn't."

"What about money though?" asked Cooper.

"We've got enough to live very comfortably on for the rest of our life. But I already have an idea how to keep an income flowing," replied Jordan.

"How, babe?" said Cooper, taking a bite of an English muffin.

"I'll just move over to the other side," smiled the lobbyist. Instead of Lower the Rainbow it will be Raise the Rainbow. Instead of Stay In it will be Come Out. In place of Remove the Grooming it will be Educate to be Awake. And guess what? In two weeks I am scheduled to actually speak before Congress to explain Stay In before they conduct a final vote. Boy are they all going to be in for a surprise."

"Come here baby," said Cooper. "Put this tray on the table there. I don't need any more of *that* kind of breakfast. I need some loving breakfast."

Chapter Nine

The congressional chambers were full to capacity on the early Monday morning Jordan Sam was one of the scheduled speakers on the proposed Stay In legislation before the House. Some observers and media immediately noticed something different about the lobbyist. He wasn't wearing his usual dark suit, white shirt, or blue tie. He had on a light lavender colored jacket and designer blue jeans, a light pink shirt with the top three buttons open. If one got close enough to the lobbyist they also spotted a small rainbow flag lapel. Chatter was already starting to roll across the aisle; some people were nervous. But none were more nervous than Jordan as he prepared to give a speech that would forever change his life. Not only that: it would change the lives of millions of Americans and even people across the world. Following a few other presenters who made their cases for and against Stay In, Jordan was introduced.

"Up next is Jordan Sam, president of the Jordan Sam Group and as primary lobbyist on this proposed bill, the underlying author of the legislation."

Seated in the front row before Congress, Jordan read from prepared notes and improvised portions of his speech.

"One of the worst things I have ever done in my sixty five years on this planet has come to haunt me today. Because of it I open with a line from a poem by Alexander Pope's "An Essay on Criticism."

To err is human, to forgive divine.

As most of you know there has been occasional speculation over the two decades spanning my career, that I might be homosexual. I have steadfastly denied it. Not only did I deny being gay, I became one of the most vocal critics of homosexuality, guiding my own company into a position of suppressing the gay movement, denying any and all who are different, from legal protection under the law, under the U.S. Constitution. But I have caught myself on the precipice of this proposed legislation, a law proposed but not yet law. It is my duty today, and I say it gives me great, proud pleasure to withdraw my support for the very bill I jump started. *Ladies and gentleman, my name is Jordan Sam and I am a homosexual.* I am gay. I am with another man and we are getting married."

Now the sagacious chamber filled with chatter, with gasps, even with a few loud cries of treason.

"Order in these chambers!" cried the Speaker of the House, banging with his gavel. "Order!"

"Out with him!" came one last cry before the room once again became silent. Jordan continued.

"I hereby remove my support and participation in not only Stay In, but for all legislation on this subject for which I was a lobby consultant. While it is not my business whether someone reveals themself as gay, lesbian, transgender, I now urge anyone who feels so compelled, to be yourself, to come out if you will. I also encourage individuals, companies, organizations to proudly display the flag that represents the struggle for gay freedom that began many decades ago in America, to fly the Rainbow Flag, to wear those colors anywhere and everywhere you so please, as I wear them today on my chest. And now comes the hardest part, explaining to you, to the world why I was such a fierce, unrelenting advocate against the rights of gays in our country. I was one of the most selfish people I know. I also had traits that although almost all of us have them from time to time, mine were on super steroids: jealousy, rage, ignorance, greed. I sold myself out for the love of money instead of the love of people. I catered to a small but powerful group who wanted to divide America because division is good for their business, good for politics, good for extreme religion. In a word, I was lonely and did not have love. I had self-hate. I didn't know it but my actions were the result of deep-seated envy. In my secret life I strove for things I thought would make me happy, and they did, for a few minutes. But real happiness comes from freedom: freedom to be yourself and to not be compelled by law to temper your so-called differentness because some people think your way of living is against the bible, against God or any other religious figure one finds around the world. I say to those people: *if that is what you believe then believe it for yourselves, for your own lives and if you are right then you will go wherever it is you say you will go when you die. It is not for you to force other people to legally not be themselves, to be like you. Why do you care about what they do?*

Imagine several school children in a classroom being taught history, being taught that a key historical figure was married and had four children. Would you not call that grooming those children - who may be gay and no one knows it - to be hetrosexual? This is as much "grooming" as pointing out in a class lecture on the subject of literature that Oscar Wilde was gay, or on the subject of musicians that Elton John is gay. If you think this is grooming school children to be gay, then maybe it's you who need to go back to school.

I was part of a powerful lobby that wants to severely restrict and in some cases outlaw being gay not because a man loves a man or a woman loves a woman or a person discovers their very brain does not match the body they were given. The truth is about politics, about money: about power. There is a fear that gays, left to openly be themselves will one day become powerful leaders in America, in the world. You've heard the cliches: gays are so smart. Gays are so witty. A lot of women love being around gays, having them as best friends. The fact is these are not just cliches, they are the truth and it's a truth the companies and organizations I worked for want to stop and stop quickly.

Gay and transgender people are not asking to be treated better than everyone else. We are asking to be treated equally. We are asking to be left alone to live our lives as you so luckily are allowed without question or resistance to live yours. We don't want to turn kids gay. I know many of you find it hard to believe God would allow someone to be born gay, so it's easier for you to reconcile that thought by claiming people choose to be gay and can be made to reverse that choice.

I can no longer be a part of a system that tries to legislate gay and transgender people to a cave of no return. I hereby formally withdraw my participation in the Stay In bill, and urge Congress to reject the legislation. Should it instead still move forward, I stand ready to battle against it. Thank you for your time and attention today, and to all I have hurt by my actions and participation in this bill and similar bills, I profusely apologize. Please remember Alexander Pope's poem and perhaps find it in your heart to forgive me."

Chapter Ten

Seven Years Later

Little Cooper Jr. looked at the slice of raisin bread on his

plate. Then he looked at Cooper and Jordan who sat with him
in the breakfast nook of their downsized New Orleans condo,
and pouted.

"Coop, The raisins are burned. Or did you make the toast,
Jordan?"

They both laughed. "Son, Cooper made that toast," replied
Jordan.

"Did not," said Cooper. "I saw Jordan make that toast with my
own eyes."

"Well,"replied the blond-haired boy, "I will say both of you
made it and I don't like it!" Then he threw the piece of toast

across the room and it landed in the garbage can. Cooper and Jordan dropped their jaws.

"Well young man,"said Jordan. "If it weren't for the fact that you actually scored two points with that throw, I would scold you and maybe even take away your tablet for a few days."

"Yeah," added Cooper,"but still, those are some bad manners, son. Please try not to do that again. We can make you another piece of toast."

"Ok, Coop," replied Cooper Jr., lowering his head.

Jordan got up from the table and walked over to the boy. "No need to be sad about it, son. It's just a piece of toast. Hey, you want to visit with Evangeline today? She said she bought you something special…"

"Yeah! Yeah! Yeah!" exclaimed Cooper Jr., knowing his billionaire birth mother would give him something awesome. After she gave birth to the boy she made an agreement with Cooper and Jordan to allow the adoption process. With the help of Jordan she reversed her anti-homosexual position and even founded The Evangeline Project, a non-profit benefiting gay couples in the long, often troubling adoption process.

"It's not that I don't love him, but it seems obvious you guys will give him a much better home. I'm just too enmeshed in my business. As long as I can see him when I want, we should be good," she said.

As it turned out that night in Le Arrondissement Hotel seven years ago left the billionairess with a human gift and made Cooper a surprised father. The timing was perfect. Jordan and Cooper had just got married and had discussed how wonderful it would be if they could adopt. In this case the adoption process was made a lot easier since Cooper was the father and did not have to jump through adoption hoops. Jordan, from his years as a lobbyist, knew the process and it made it easier for him to get through it all. The couple decided early on to avoid the confusion that the mommy-daddy scenario would inevitably bring since they were both men, so they started by identifying by their first names. Cooper Jr. would not have to wonder who is mommy, who is daddy and all the confusing reasons why his situation didn't match his play and schoolmates. There would come a time soon when they would have the "talk" with the boy, when he was old enough to understand they were a couple, two men in love and married and although it was not the so-called traditional marriage, it was a legal and binding marriage just the same.

Not long after they were married, Jordan helped Cooper open his own towing company, aptly named Cooper Towing, Inc. Through connections with "important people" in New Orleans Jordan helped his husband secure a lucrative Mardi Gras contract and almost three quarters of his annual income was earned in just that two week period. Jordan had become a respected gay rights lobbyist, with his Rainbow Rights legislation making it all the way to the Supreme Court, who ruled 5-4 in favor of the right for the rainbow flag to be flown in public places including schools. Life was not just good - it was great. After they left Cooper Jr. with Evangeline for the night, the couple had a drink on their French Quarter condo balcony. Cooper fell into a sort of melancholic reminiscence on his past.

"I mean, when I really think about some of the things I said - and did, I look at me now and ask myself who was that guy? Was that really me?"

"Yeah babe," said Cooper. "You were a card back then. But then again so was I. I was in the deepest kind of gay denial imaginable. The totally straight wrecker driver who liked plowing chicks. Then I eventually graduated to letting you go down on me but I was still straight, right?"

Jordan took a sip of his drink and ran his fingers through his now thinning hair. He was 72 years old now and Coop was only 37. He felt lucky to have such a young husband.

"And the funny thing is I loved the idea of you being totally straight. Since I was denying gay rights and hated other queers, that's all I wanted was a straight man. And I was the very queen of size queens. I was the queen of closets. Remember that time I flew to Ecuador because the men there supposedly have the biggest ones in the world?"

"Yep," replied Cooper. "That's probably why you and me got back together. I saved you from there. You had a little nervous breakdown. But at least you did get one fringe benefit from it all."

"What's that?" replied Jordan.

With a sly smile Cooper reached down and grabbed himself.

"This 14."

"Hmm," replied Jordan, scooting his chair closer to his husband as they watched the sun set over the Quarter.

"We've got the place to ourselves tonight," said Jordan. "Do you happen to have your measuring tape with you? I need to double-check and make sure you really are 14."

Cooper reached to the belt wrapped around his dark blue work pants and unclipped his measuring tape.

"Oh it's 14 all right. But if you make a cup of your famous hot chamomile tea, it might even prove to be 15."

"15 it is," laughed Jordan, almost tripping over himself to get the teapot on the stove.

The End

Preston Brady III is the author of several novels and non-fiction books, including gay novels *Pole Polishers* and *A Love So Blue*. He attended college in San Francisco where he lived for 14 years, and currently resides in his home state of Alabama. He loves cats and dogs, walking, beaches, fine cuisine and world travel.

www.ingramcontent.com/pod-product-compliance
Lightning Source LLC
Chambersburg PA
CBHW072029170626
46811CB00008B/2994